MORE CHRISTMAS GHOST STORIES

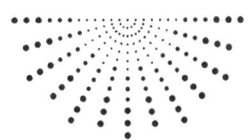

TONY WALKER

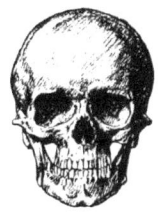

I would like to thank my beta-readers for their suggestions, corrections and inspiration.

Brad Hamann
Gary Johnston
Rebecca Katz
Steph Newham
Mark Zeiger

CONTENTS

1. Nuremberg Christmas Market   1
2. Surprise View   10
3. North Sea 3 a.m   21
4. The Snow Globe   27
5. The Patron Saint of Thieves   36
6. Music From Another Room   54
7. The Lights   74
8. The Hitcher   87
9. An Edinburgh Ghost Story   94

About the Author   115
Also by Tony Walker   117

1
NUREMBERG CHRISTMAS MARKET

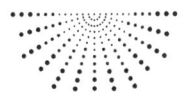

*W*e cross from Dover on the ferry and get some time to stretch our legs in Holland before it's back on the bus. The sinking sun stains the sky to the west as the engine starts, and we're off on the the long haul to Germany.

Now it's very dark. Emma sleeps beside me as the bus hums down the autobahn. Her breath sighs in and out. I wipe condensation from the window to see what I can see, but it's not much—just a red glow from invisible cities strung along the Rhine: Nijmegen, Cologne, Koblenz.

Dim red lights run along the length of the bus, not enough to read by, just enough to stop people tripping over.

We consume miles and minutes, and minutes and more miles. Murmuring drifts down from the driver and the relief driver up at the front, and the scrunching sound of someone eating crisps comes from behind. I have no idea where we are.

I want it all to be nice for Emma. She loves Christmas. She loves the lights and the joy of it, and she deserves that joy too.

Finally, I fall asleep. I dream of nothing and jerk awake as the bus stops. I sit up. 'What?'

Emma leans in to kiss my cheek.

I make a joke of it. What? Where? When? Eh?'

'You were asleep,' she laughs.

I groan. 'It's allowed. It's night.'

'It's about ten o'clock.'

'Only ten? I feel like we've been driving forever.'

'Me too.'

The coach is still mainly dark. Some people have put on the overhead reading lights, and pools of white dot the length of the coach, but most still sleep or try to.

I say, 'What've we stopped for?'

'Change of drivers, I think, and a pee break.'

I peer from the window. We're at a motorway service station. I rub the condensation to look out better at parked lorries and lines of cars. There are some people about. There's a Burger King, and a petrol station lit up down a way. 'Where are we?'

'Cologne?' She snuggles into me. 'Not sure.'

We're headed down to Bavaria—the Christmas Market at Nuremberg. It's supposed to be the best in Germany, and if it's the best Christmas Market in Germany, it's the best in Europe and probably the world.

In the low light, it's hard to see if she looks ill. I always worry. We don't know anything, but given the family history, we expect the worst. Not that she's letting it show. She's lovely. She always is to me.

We stop at Frankfurt for breakfast and hang around to get a mug of German coffee, bratwurst and mustard and more Stollen cake, just because we can. We then stop in Wurzburg.

The Germans know how to do Christmas. The whole country is like a Coca Cola advert. We arrive at Nuremberg by early evening, booked into a delightful hotel. The plan is a look around the big Christmas Market this evening, something to eat then back on the coach. We're going to stop tomorrow at Bruges before getting the ferry back to England the day after. A whistle-stop tour indeed.

Emma turns up her collar and tightens her scarf as we leave the hotel. She has her woolly hat and gloves on. It's cold, just as it should be.

The evening gathers itself as we stroll around the Medieval Town, reconstructed so beautifully to create a dream of a German Gothic past, deep in the Bavarian forest, with castles and towers and city walls.

There are little cafes with Black Forest gateaux soaked in kirsch. The shops glitter and sparkle with fairy lights. The air is cold, but the Glühwein fortified with schnapps warms the cockles of my heart. Emma is laughing so much. She loves it.

I smell warm cinnamon twirls and sugary candy-floss. We stroll and stop at stalls with wooden figures of soldiers and dancers, and a mouse with a sword all glittered with gold spins from a loop on a Christmas tree.

There are baubles and spangles and glass that shines and sparkles in the myriad coloured lights. Clouds of breath and sounds of laughter fill the air while tourists trot round the town square sitting in old-fashioned lacquered carriages pulled by sleepy horses.

Top-hatted gipsies drive them, not needing to use the whips that loll in their hand: the horses know the way. The drivers smile and tip their hats and nod to wide-eyed tourist boys and girls, and to tourist men and women too in the hope of a fare.

Emma and I find magic lantern stalls, and stalls selling Stolen cake and more mulled wine, and the most marvellous Christmas paper covered in reindeers and stars. It's all there to be bought, and Emma is so happy, that I don't mind buying it. I will spend the money. There will always be more money.

I can speak a bit of German. Not fluently, but I like the language and can make myself understood.

I give in to a top-hatted driver and Emma climbs in to take a trip around Nuremberg Old Town. The carriage creaks with leather and wood as the springs jolt and the two horses move off.

Emma asks the driver what the horses are called. He's Romanian, I think, not German, but he says, 'Dietrich and Kaspar,' and he asks us where we're from, and do we like Nuremberg? Emma answers before I can, 'I love it. It's magical.'

We get out at the end, and I pay and Emma strokes Dietrich and

Kaspar and the driver, Petru from Sibiu, allows her to give them an apple each which he has stocked up for the purpose. That's another sly Euro or two between him and me behind Emma's back, but she feeds the horses as they crunch the apples from her outstretched palms.

WE EAT GOULASH with Bavarian bread and dark German beer in a lovely hotel called *Zum Schwartzen Käfer*. The other members of our party are gathered around chatting. We hardly know them, but we're friends until we depart at Dover never to meet again. The thought comes to me that I might meet them next Christmas, but I dismiss the thought. I wouldn't come on anything like this excursion on my own.

I glance at Emma. She's red-cheeked and happy, so I order more beer. In other times she might tell me not to drink so much, but she just smiles at me and strokes the back of my hand.

I've had schnapps and mulled wine and beer and more beer, and I wouldn't normally drink this much, but I'm on holiday, and it helps quieten the awful gnawing in my guts.

I feel out of the conversation. I just watch Emma chat, and then I see a man standing at the entrance to the dining room. He's staring at me. Weirdly, he's dressed in motorcycle leathers. He has a helmet in his hand, hanging down by the chinstrap. He flickers like a movie projected onto smoke, like an image on rippling muslin. He's tall. He looks like a normal young man apart from the rippling.

But he's a ghost. I've seen them before.

I used to see ghosts all the time when I was a kid. When I was out with my friends in bars as a teenager, they would gather around me wanting to pass on messages to their loved ones, wanting someone to talk to. I never mentioned it.

My grandmother was what they call 'A Wise Woman' in our village way up in rural Cumbria, so maybe it's a gift that runs in the family, but it's not a gift I wanted. Eventually, when I stopped listening to them, the spirits stopped talking to me. I preferred it that way. I didn't want to be known as a weirdo who spoke to the dead.

But this German boy doesn't go away. He stands in his leathers with his helmet. The waiters and guests going in and out to the toilet, walk past him, not paying him any attention, but weirdly they step around him as if avoiding something they can't see but sense.

He stares at me and stares at me. Inside my mind, I mutter, 'Go away,' but he doesn't leave. I'm growing angry. I don't want to be disturbed on my last holiday with Emma. Emma, who is so happy now. There I've said it: that's what I fear. We don't even know it's terminal. They can treat it these days much better. Her mother and grandmother died of it, but that was years ago. I shouldn't be so negative.

And the boy stands there like he needs me to listen. Blonde hair, and young face—maybe seventeen or eighteen? And thinking of Emma, my heart melts. What if there's something I can do? That's probably the alcohol talking, but I feel suddenly emotional. I'll help anyone, any creature living or dead, in the hope that someone will help my Emma.

As I walk towards him, he walks away. He leads me to the door of the hotel, past the crowd of guests all having a good time. The cold air sobers me a little. He waits for me and says 'Please help me.'

I shake my head to clear it. I haven't talked to one of these things for so long.

'I am Peter,' he says 'I lived near here once. Just a short walk.'

I sigh. 'What do you want me to do?' I've decided to do it, it seems.

'My mother. Her heart is broken. I want you to tell her I'm all right.'

I breathe in heavily. 'I don't know your mother.'

'It doesn't matter. I'll show you where she is.'

This is nuts. I'm talking to someone immaterial, agreeing to run an errand for him.

He says, 'Not many people can see me. I sensed you could.'

I'm about to explain that I used to see people, that it's something in my family, that it's nothing I want anything to do with any more, but he stands there—a young man in motorcycle leathers. I don't even know if we're speaking English or German.

As if reading my thoughts, he says, 'An accident. Just coming out of town. The lorry driver didn't look.'

'How long?' I ask.

'Nearly two years. I am not bounded by time anymore like you are. Mother has grieved too long too much. She needs to be able to be happy again.'

I rub my forehead. 'I need to tell my wife that I'm going.'

'Don't worry. She won't know.'

'How?'

'It doesn't matter. But thank you. Come now. It will be quick.'

When we're halfway there, he turns and says, 'Just tell her I'm happy and not to worry, and that I'll see her again.'

I follow him as he walks through the streets of the old town, past the stalls and the lights, past the sparkles and warmth which get more distant and colder as if I am wandering through a netherworld of shadows and memories. I sense other ghosts around me, noticing me, paying attention, wanting to speak, but they respect Peter and let me pass unmolested.

I can't say how long I walk, or how far it is. But the house I stand outside now is a modern one. It's what we would call a Council House in England, very modest, dating from the 1980s maybe—not old, not spooky: nothing out of the ordinary at all.

Peter waits beside me. He's waiting to see if I'll help him.

I have an attack of the nerves. I don't know. This is nuts. What will the woman say, if I turn up out of the blue like this. To her, I'm just a weird Englishman who tells her, 'Excuse me, you don't know me, but I've just seen your dead son, and he asked me to tell you...'

She'll very likely call the police and get me committed to a lunatic asylum.

Peter stands, the shadows whirling around us. It's cold. My lips are dry, my mouth thick.

'Knock,' he says.

'How can I?'

Long seconds drift by. 'Please?' he says.

He seems close to despair. I don't know if it's fear or embarrassment or plain cowardice, but I can't knock.

Then I feel his sad eyes on me. This seventeen-year-old boy killed far too young.

'Okay,' I say and rap on the door. It stings my knuckles even though the rap is so quiet. She'll never hear that. I know it.

I clear my throat and knock again, harder this time. A third time, then I see a bell that I could have rung, but she's already coming.

A lady, maybe fifty years old, with dyed blonde hair, quite tall. She looks at me in puzzlement and with a little fear. What on earth am I doing at her doorstep?

'Hallo?' she asks.

'Entshuldigung,' I begin in German. 'Ich heisse Keith Malory. Ich bin...'

'English?' she asks.

I nod gratefully.

'Can I help you?' she says.

I clear my throat again. This is going to be difficult. I say, 'I know this will be hard to believe. I'm a tourist here, Keith Malory, but I see... In my family, there's what they call "the sight". Do you know what I mean?'

She doesn't, so I laboriously explain. Eventually, she gets a glimmer. She looks worried now. She wants me to leave and is looking for any opportunity to close the door. Luckily the Germans are so polite.

Peter is gone. I can't see him anymore, so there's just his mother and me.

Finally, I say, 'Your son, Peter...'

Her eyes fill up. She catches at her throat.

I continue. 'I saw him. He spoke to me.'

She says nothing, just keeps staring at me with a mixture of horror, wonder and hope.

I say, 'He wants you to know he's happy. Try not to worry about him.'

She breaks down in tears. I wonder if she's going to slap me, but then she looks up, wiping streaming tears from her cheeks and eyes. 'I'm sorry I have no handkerchief.'

I say, 'Don't worry. I'm sorry I came to tell you this. It's so strange, I know. I hope you're not angry with me.'

She composes herself. 'No, Mr Malory. I am not angry with you.'

Then, and it's definitely wonder now. 'You saw him?'

'Yes.'

'How did he look?'

She has a thousand questions I can't answer. All I know is that he wanted me to tell her that he was fine and she should grieve no more.

She nods at the end, and we go silent. It's awkward. I want to leave to get back to Emma. She'll be wondering where I've got to.

'Can I give you money?' Peter's mother suddenly asks. 'I am so grateful.'

I wave it away. 'No, I don't need anything. I'm just sorry to have to come to you with such a strange message. It must be peculiar.'

'I'm not sorry,' she says. 'I want to thank you so much, but you won't take money.'

'No.' I'm about to leave when she suddenly rushes into the house and comes back with a silver star, the sort you put on a Christmas Tree. But it's small; it would fit in the palm of your hand.

She says 'It was his. He had his own tree as a boy. He loved Christmas.'

'I couldn't possibly,' I say.

But she replies, 'No. It is the star of hope. You have given me back hope.'

I stumble away into the dark. I put the star into the pocket of my coat. I don't know where I am, and then I see him standing in a dark corner.

'Thank you,' he says quietly.

'She gave me your star.'

He smiles. 'You're welcome to it. Thank you. We won't meet again.'

I'm sorry, but I'm glad too.

'It's that way,' he says, pointing back to the Old Town. I can hear the noise of the market now and the fairground with its Merry Go Round of painted horses.

I back away from him, and am about to turn when he says, 'I just wanted to thank you for your kind act and tell you that Emma will live. Don't worry.'

EMMA THINKS I've been to the toilet. She's been having a good time and hasn't noticed I've been gone for so long. We get back on the bus, and by midnight we're zooming along the autobahn heading for Belgium and Bruges, passing all the twinkling lights of Germany.

Emma falls asleep, lulled by the mulled wine and the warm talk and glittering lights. I watch her breathe slowly in the humming dark of the coach. Long miles stretch out, and still, I watch her sleep.

I think my interlude with Peter was a dream. It seems so unreal. Maybe I dozed off on my seat in the hotel and dreamt it all.

And I watch Emma and worry, because I always worry about her these days, what with the tests and the doctors.

But then my fingers feel their way into the pocket of my coat that now lies folded over Emma and me to keep us warm, and I feel the prickle of the silver star.

2

SURPRISE VIEW

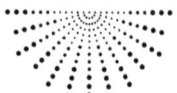

Dust as we are, the immortal spirit grows...

From The Prelude, *William Wordsworth*

*E*arly evening, but it's dark already: a winter's night. A wine bar in Soho, and a man sits nursing a balloon glass of red wine. He was once an English teacher, and is now a banker.

A woman comes in. Lots of women and men come in, but he's waiting for this one. He stands, smiles, and pulls out a chair for her. She gives him a light kiss on both cheeks. He seems preoccupied, sad even, but he puts on a brave face and greets her with affection.

'Sorry, I'm late,' she says, hand on his shoulder.

'No problem, Helen. I had my friends to keep me company.' He nods at the wine glass, and Helen sees the bottle that stands beside it, two-thirds empty.

He sees her looking. 'I'll get another bottle,' but she puts up a hand. 'No, I'm fine with that.' She points to the remains of the wine. She's probably thinking that her having some will stop him drinking it all himself.

They both sit. After a minute, she says softly. 'The wine...'

He sighs and shrugs. 'I know.'

'I know it's been hard. I don't mean to nag, but alcohol is a medicine that turns into a poison.' She's a psychiatrist, works for the South London and Maudsley Hospital Trust with patients who abuse alcohol and drugs.

He smiles. 'You're my big sister. You're just looking out for me.' He pours her a glass of wine and finishes the bottle himself, filling his glass with an apologetic, but insincere smile.

'How've you been?' she asks kindly.

'So, so.'

She places her hand on top of his. 'I'm so sorry. I can't even imagine...'

His mouth goes tight. 'Neither could I, but I don't have to imagine now.' He thinks he's being self-pitying and forces a smile, realises that's inappropriate, then his face falls into emptiness. He wears an expression that neither expresses his feelings nor hides them.

Helen says, 'She was lovely. It's so sad.'

'Sad for both of them.'

'Of course,' she says softly. 'For both of them.'

The funerals are now over. Brother and sister know what happened well enough, so instead they talk about his plans for Christmas.

'You're coming to ours, David,' Helen says firmly.

He grimaces. 'I think I'll just go away somewhere on my own. I don't want to be at home.'

'Please, Mike's looking forward to talking to you about football. It's the only male company he gets.'

David rubs his eyes. 'I don't know.'

Silence. Helen thinks about the family Christmas. David thinks about the wind and the rain and the dark skies full of clouds.

He winces. 'It's just I think I'd be better on my own.'

She purses her lips. 'I'm not sure you would.'

In the night outside, a whirl of snowflakes blows along Greek Street. David watches as, in the yellow streetlight, they twist, whirl and melt. He lifts his glass to his lips, sips.

His sister watches him.

He says, 'I was thinking of Cumbria.'

'The Lake District?'

'Yes, near Keswick. Borrowdale Valley.'

'Among strangers?'

'Strangers soon become friends. She used to say that.'

Two days before Christmas: David has his room in the Borrowdale Hotel booked for a Christmas and New Year package. He doesn't know if he'll stay for New Year, but you had to book it that way.

Today, he's walking up to Watendlath. The air is crisp and cold with the clouds coloured the soft white that forecasts snow. David trudges up through the woods, crunching ice in the puddles. All around are moss-covered rocks and the trees—pines, oak and ash. A squirrel darts above him from branch to branch. He hardly catches a glance of it but thinks it was a Red.

A sudden break in the trees shows the Derwent Fells to his left. He's nearly at Ashness Bridge now. When he gets to the old stone bridge, there's a Mountain Goat bus stopped and a cargo of visitors: Chinese, Japanese, Indian and Mancunians are smiling and taking snaps of themselves on the stone arch—the most photographed bridge in the Lake District.

The beck froths and frets, plunging down between rocks all the way to the lake below. A glance up shows Derwentwater and beyond, Skiddaw looming iced in snow like a huge Stollen cake.

Beautiful, but it still can't take the grief away. His wife was killed while driving at speed to see their son who'd been rushed into hospital with viral meningitis. It was a double funeral. She was on her own because he was still at work, making money: money, money, money. Lots of money. Enough money to buy the moon maybe, but not enough to bring you back the ones you love—the ones you love and who've now gone where you can never see them again.

And then David re-enters the woods. The trees stand bare-leaved and stark in the still winter air, trunk after trunk after trunk, mesmerising. David walks through the trees and is surprised by the view: Surprise View. It is aptly named.

The naked apron of rock is a popular beauty spot. It overlooks the lake far below and stands opposite the mountains, across an echo of cold air. Beautiful, but it still doesn't take the biting, numbing grief away. The view of the trees just brings memories. The sound of the wind just brings memories. The smell of the damp earth just brings memories, and they were never even here, never in Cumbria, that's why he chose to come here. Never here, and not anywhere now.

David leaves the lake view and walks on, again lost in the trees, trudging over gravel and ice. His breath comes out in clouds—and then the snow begins to fall—not heavily, just a fluttering, just a touch of soft flakes that come spiralling down through the trees, landing on fallen branches and clumps of moss, dusting them with such delicacy, half melting, half remaining.

Soft, soft, soft. The gentle caress of the snow on his face. The air becomes confiding and cold, wrapping the woods in silence. There's nobody here now. The tourists, like his wife and son, have gone. There's just his own breath, the feel of his heart in his chest and the soft sound of his boots on the forest floor.

He stands alone—the last man on earth. And then he sees the stag. It's seen him first, of course, standing fifty yards away. The magnificent beast, shaggy red-brown with five tines on its antlers, watches him quietly. The stag stares impassively and David meets its stare. The black of the animal's eye draws him in. The world stops spinning. For a brief, epiphany moment the man, the stag, the universe are one, and David knows he's made from the same stuff as the stag, as the wood, as the wind itself.

A line from William Wordsworth's *Prelude* comes unexpectedly into David's head:

"I had melancholy thoughts...
   a strangeness in my mind,
   A feeling that I was not for that hour,
   Nor for that place."

13

The reverie is suddenly broken. The stag scents something and lifts its head and looks into the wood, a flutter of snow between him and it now. Then the stag breaks into a trot and disappears further into the forest.

David stands quietly, still transfixed by what he has just seen and felt.

From behind, he hears the sound of a horn, as if from far away. Riders appear. Slowly, they emerge from some dream of winter long ago. The horsemen pick their way through the trees, the clip, clump of horses' hooves, their snorts and billowing clouds of breath. Men and beasts look ghostly in the falling snow like the companions of King Arthur or John Peel.

There are women on some of the horses. They come close but don't speak, drifting like spectres through the wood, the snow falling on them. Not enough to settle, but enough to land on cheeks and eyelashes. The riders go on in silence, the dogs trotting by the horses and then a woman speaks from behind.

She's mounted on a chestnut horse with a white blaze on its nose. David turns, startled by her sudden appearance as she appears like a spirit from between the dark-boled trees.

'I didn't mean to surprise you.' The woman is well-spoken, the accent standard English, not the Northern that they speak round here.

David says, 'Are you one of the hunters?' He's prepared to get into an argument.

The woman has long grey hair, pulled back in a ponytail. Her face is high-cheeked, and she must be in her sixties, if not older—her eyes, pale-brown, look down on him, a ghost of a smile on her face.

'No. I don't ride with the hunt,' she says.

'But you're on horseback.'

Her smile broadens. 'It's not against the law.'

Something about her challenges him, and he still wants to argue. He's still angry. 'Isn't it dangerous riding among the trees, with all these rocks and fallen branches?'

'The horse knows his way.'

There's nothing offensive about the woman, but rage boils in

David's chest, the unfairness of her being so serene and him feeling like all his skin is cut away. He is prepared to shout about hunting, though she's no hunter. It's just a coincidence that she's riding in the wood. But it's crazy, riding in a wood. She should know better.

The woman goes on. 'I live near here with my husband. He's a doctor.'

David waits. He doesn't know what to say. He wishes she'd leave, but then she says as if she's been working up her courage. 'There is always forever, you know.'

David is irritable, unaccountably so, but the woman rides on, and he watches her go. He loses sight of her amongst the trees, her strange departing words echo in his head.

Later, he passes a house. It's old, made of Lakeland slate. It's called Grey Crag and looks like it could belong to a doctor and a posh lady who rides horses through the woods. A Christmas tree glistens in the window—red and white and blue lights, gold tinsel twined among dark green needles, a golden star gleaming on the very top.

David walks on.

BACK AT THE bar after his walk, he feels the glow of the fire. Standing there, he orders a bottle of wine.

'Two glasses?' the barman asks.

'One will be fine.' Then he takes the bottle and the glass and finds a table near the open fire, roasting his face in the heat. It feels good. It's the only thing that feels good. The fire, and maybe the wine, but he drinks it too fast to taste it. It's an insult to an excellent wine to be gulped like this, but the liquor takes away his memories and his grief. For a while, at least. At least until 2 am when he'll roll awake as if he's never slept. Sweating from alcohol, weeping from a heartbreak never to be fixed.

David stares into the fire, glass in his fist. A man appears next to him.

'Mind if I sit here?'

David grunts. 'No.' It's instinctive, but he looks around. There are other tables, but they're all occupied. People are arriving for dinner, having a drink in the bar first.

'Are you having dinner?' the man asks. He looks to be around seventy. Dressed in a tweed jacket with leather patches at the elbows, short grey hair, glasses and a grey moustache.

'David nods at his wine glass. 'That.'

'Oh dear,' says the man, overstepping the bounds of politeness, those unwritten rules meant to keep strangers from commenting on your behaviour; no matter how self-destructive.

'Sorry,' the man says, extending a hand. David pauses, then unclamps his fist from the wine-glass and limply shakes the proffered hand. 'David Peat,' he says.

The older man smiles. 'John Hand.' He nods at the wine. 'Used to be my business—health. I'm a retired GP.'

David says, 'My sister works in the field. With addictions. Down in London.'

'Ah, up here on holiday?'

'Sort of.'

'With your family?'

'I don't have any family.'

It could have meant anything, but the doctor knows it instantly. He's gentle. 'Sorry.'

David looks back at his wine. 'You didn't know. Not your fault.'

The doctor goes silent and David, sensing the unspoken question, says, 'I had a son. He was eighteen. He died. My wife died around the same time.'

'I'm very sorry to hear that.'

'Again, not your fault.' He takes another mouthful of wine.

'There is no time, you know. Nothing is lost if you look with your heart rather than your eyes.'

'Really.' David pushes his hand through his hair. 'What does that even mean?'

The doctor meets his eye. 'I lost my wife. In a riding accident.'

'I'm sorry to hear that,' David says. He's staring into the fire now.

'She shouldn't have been riding there. I often told her. When she went, my heart broke. I didn't know what to do. I even sold the house. I couldn't bear to be there without her. I came and moved in here.'

David raises an eyebrow. 'To this hotel?'

Dr Hand nods. 'I've been here ever since.'

'That must cost you a fortune.'

'I knew the original owner. He's dead now. But we had an arrangement, and I was fortunate enough that money was no object at the time.'

'Nor to me, but it doesn't help, does it?'

Dr Hand shakes his head sadly and looks kindly at David. He goes on. 'I came to see that all time is eternally present. All of our memories, all of those we have loved are as close to us as a whisper. We just don't perceive them. Nothing needs to be saved, because nothing is truly lost.'

David says softly, 'It's kind of you to say that. I appreciate you trying to comfort me, but I feel so alone. I feel I've lost them forever. That they're gone, and I'm here alone forever.'

'But that can't be so,' Hand says. 'Don't you see?'

David shakes his head and sinks into reverie. When he looks up again, the doctor has gone.

CHRISTMAS EVE: no snow, but it's a bright frosty morning. The desk clerk says, 'Another walk today, Mr Peat? You'll be very fit!'

David says. 'I'll be back for dinner.' For some reason, he slept better last night, and he feels lighter than he has since his wife and son died. At first, that seems like a betrayal, but he knows they wouldn't want him sad. Wherever they are.

He walks a different way round. At last, he finds himself in the wood where he saw the stag. He stands a while, looking out for it, the memory of their shared moment together still fresh in his mind's eye. But the stag does not return.

At Surprise View, he stops to gaze at the mountains and the lakes. You can see up the chain of valleys all the way to Scotland, clear and bright over the narrow sea. He feels strikingly, blindingly alone, but now it matters less. He's alone, but somehow not alone. Something the doctor said has struck home: 'Nothing needs to be saved, because nothing is truly lost.'

And then he walks again. He's lost in the mystery of the woods. The trees crowd around him, and once again, he feels the silence as if he's wrapped in it. He comes across the house—Grey Crag—still blazing with its Christmas tree in the window. He wonders if that's where Dr Hand, used to live.

And then he sees the lady on the chestnut horse with the blaze. She's coming through the woods, and again he thinks how dangerous it must be to take a horse over this rough terrain. Horse and rider reach the side of the house, and David steps back into the shadows so she won't see him. He wants to see where she's going. She goes around the side of the house, but before she disappears, she dismounts. She gets off the horse and clasps its reins in her gloved hand. David thinks this must be where she lives, in this old house, deep in the woods, far away from everybody, and he believes it would be a wonderful place to live with its beautiful Christmas Tree burning in the window like hope.

But she knows he's watching. She raises a silent hand in greeting, and he waves back.

BACK AT THE HOTEL, it's time for dinner. David stands at the bar. The barman who has a face like creased leather and looks like he's been working behind that bar for a thousand years asks, 'Usual bottle, Mr Peat?'

David is about to say yes.

The barman reaches to fetch a fresh bottle, but David stops him. 'Just a glass tonight, I think.'

The barman nods and fills a glass from a bottle of house red that is already open. David runs his finger round the base of the glass, but doesn't pick it up.

The barman says, 'Walked anywhere nice today?'

'Just around the fells and then back through Watendlath Woods.'

'That's a nice walk.'

David says, 'Yes, I saw a lovely Christmas tree in the window of the house up there.'

The barman raises an eyebrow. 'In the woods? I didn't know there was a house in the woods.'

'Yes, Grey Crag. It's a grand old building.'

The barman shakes his head. 'No, it can't have been Grey Crag.'

'Why not?'

'That old house is a ruin. It's been empty for twenty years. The roof's in and all.'

David grunts. 'Really? I just wondered if it had belonged to Dr Hand. The fellow that moved in here when his wife died.'

'Dr Hand? Dr John Hand?'

'Yes, that's him.'

The barman gives a surreptitious look at the wine glass in David's hand, still untouched. Finally, he patiently explains, 'You can't have met Dr Hand.'

David frowns. 'But I did. Here. Last night.'

The barman says, 'He was here when I first came. Lived here for a couple of years. I believe his wife was thrown from her horse in the woods. He couldn't live in the house after that and left it.'

David remembers the woman rider. That is strange, but the story was the one the doctor told him. He asks, 'Well if he doesn't live here anymore, he must live nearby because he was in this bar with me last night.'

The barman says firmly, 'Dr Hand died over fifteen years ago. I know, because I went to his funeral at the little church in the valley.'

And then David remembers what the doctor had said: Nothing is lost: Everything is eternally present if you just look with your heart, not your eyes. The dead do return.

The hotel manager passes. 'No rush,' he says, 'but I've got the Christmas Day menu here if you want to choose.'

David smiles. The manager listens while David says, 'No, thanks. You've been wonderfully kind, but I'm going back down to London to spend Christmas with my sister and her family.'

He leaves the wine untouched.

> *But thou art with us, with us in the past,*
> *The present, with us in the times to come.*
> *There is no grief, no sorrow, no despair,*
> *No languor, no dejection, no dismay,*
> *No absence scarcely can there be, for those*
> *Who love as we do.*

William Wordsworth.

3

NORTH SEA 3 A.M

I couldn't sleep. The ferry rolled and heaved its way across the North Sea from Amsterdam to Newcastle. Deep down in its iron belly, Sally and I lay in our twin beds. I heard her gentle breathing from across the cabin, but as I say, I couldn't sleep.

It was hot. I heard the cars shift in the decks around and below us and a car alarm ringing a long way off, muffled by bulkheads of steel. I had earplugs in, but I could still hear the ship's engine throbbing. Even so, it wasn't the noise that kept me awake.

I wasn't anxious or ill, I just couldn't sleep. Whether it was the movement, the incessant drone of the massive engines, or the heat, or a combination of them all, I don't know. Damn it, but I couldn't sleep.

I had to get up. In the faint light from under the cabin door, I pulled on my clothes, putting feet into my jeans and dragging my jumper over my head quietly so as not to wake Sally. I picked up my book. Then I let myself out. The corridor with its lines of closed doors stretched away, bathed in neon light. The carpet had seen better days, but what do you expect on a North Sea ferry ship, plying its way endlessly from port to port always full of special-offer travellers?

I was on Deck 2. I checked my watch. It was 2:10 a.m, and there was no one about. I reached the lifts and pressed the button. The lift car came down with a mechanical whirr and then a ping. The door hissed opened and the diamond above the door turned green.

The interior was mirrored on three sides. It was odd seeing the back of my head and the whorl of hair I didn't know I had. I was also going rather grey. There I was disappearing into eternity: a tired middle-aged man in an infinite regress of mirrors.

The lift's arrival at Deck 7 cut short my reveries. The door glided open, and I stepped out into the lobby area. The reception was unmanned. A crew member's jacket lay slung over a chair, and a bottle of water sat on the desk. The staff were probably in the back asleep.

The Christmas tree lights silently flashed and tinsel quietly glittered with golden fire as it stirred in a breeze that oozed in with a groan from round the metal doors.

I imagined the miles of empty sea and the wind moving over it unseen and unpeopled. The gale force wind gusted and moaned outside while the ship rolled under my feet, pitching and heaving. I kept my balance by shifting my weight like a clown on a unicycle.

The mute reception bell gleamed, silver, but why would I call anyone? I had what I needed in my glasses and my book.

Laughter echoed from the decks above. A handful of drunks were still up. Somewhere out of sight, youngsters were having a good time, laughter and conversation peppered with casual profanities in thick Newcastle accents. I didn't want to see them or, in fact, see anybody. I wanted this huge ship and the dark sea outside all to myself.

I stepped gingerly, bracing myself against the swell and headed along to the breakfast area, one hand on the counter. I passed through the empty bar, a metal screen down to protect the alcohol. The chairs had all been straightened, though old bubble-stained glasses sat here and there on tables, and a woman's glittery jacket hung on the back of a chair.

The coffee area was through the bar and also shut up. Another Christmas Tree stood here and more tinsel around the windows. I chose to sit at the far end by the door that led to the deck. I wanted to be as far away as possible from other people. I didn't want to have to chat about nothing much. I'd rather read. So I lodged myself in a corner with the North Sea at my back. I got myself comfortable, took out my book, a collection of ghost stories, placed my glasses on my nose and began to read.

The story was *They* by Rudyard Kipling, and it absorbed me into its descriptions of by-gone England in the summertime. Outside the gale screamed, and the door shifted and clicked, as the wind fretted at it.

In front of me, through the empty coffee lounge and the vacant bar leading to a deserted reception area, Christmas trees rippled through a repertoire of red and blue and yellow lights. The tinsel shimmered. The stars on top glittered silently.

But the lights' spiralling colours were an illusion: nothing really moved but the sea, and the ship on it.

Of a sudden, as I sat engrossed in stories of midnight and spirits and the shivering dead, the door came open behind, and as it opened, the sea air entered.

I put down my book. The door's movement unsettled me. It was like it was alive. I studied it, trying to calm my strange fear. Why should I be scared of a door? The bulkhead around it was painted with a red line. I supposed it was to make it more visible in case of an emergency, but it actually gave it the odd look of a mouth with the red paint acting like some freakish lipstick.

I laughed at myself, took off my glasses and rubbed my eyes. My book lay on the table in front of me: the ghost stories must be getting under my skin. I glanced out through the window for reassurance. There were lights on the deck, but they were weak against the enormous darkness outside. But no man-shaped shadows lurked there, and certainly, none had entered.

Though the door had clicked closed again, impulsively, I stepped up, steadied myself against the heavy bulkhead and shoved. I had to push my shoulder against the door to open it. I had a strange urge to breathe salt air, to step through the metal hole, as if the door beckoned me to use it.

As I opened the door, I realised I was heaving against the wind. In that case, how had the wind opened the door outwards?

Outside, the weather howled. Spray drenched me and took my breath away. It was freezing, and the sky was vast and dark and endless. I went to the white-painted rail of the deck and peered down to the waves so far below. White sea boiled while the ship ploughed its way back to England. The captain had said the weather was so rough that he would cut west from Holland to the coast of East Anglia and then follow the cliff line up to Newcastle.

Gazing out, I wondered where we were now. I could see nothing, just the North Sea stretching to an unseen horizon. No stars showed behind a covering of cloud.

And below the waves plunged, and the ship heaved, and I had the odd feeling that something waited.

It occurred to me that it would be easy to kill myself. I could just jump. There was no one around to save me, or even see me, and the sea would be so cold. Soon, I'd be abandoned, left behind by the ship and alone in a thousand miles of water a hundred fathoms deep.

I shuddered: not like me to think of suicide. It must be the ghost book getting to me again. I returned to my seat in the coffee area and sat. It was warm and strangely calming being in here with no one while the storm raged outside.

But was there no one?

And as I flicked through pages, that door kept coming open. I had the sense of it waiting for something. Once, I looked at it and it was even more mouthlike; a hungry mouth at that. I half thought I heard it whisper, muttering words I couldn't make out: the voices of all the souls the door had eaten. I shuddered. That was a stupid thought.

I was just being foolish again. Of course I was. What an imagination I'd always had. I went back to my book, but as if it was listening to me the door clicked open again. I glanced over my shoulder, and saw the door shut itself.

I muttered, 'Just the wind, just the wind, just the wind.'

There was something about that door. It frightened me, but I resolved to be brave. I pushed my glasses up my nose and read on.

After ten minutes one of the crew appeared. He walked down the deck through the bar and the coffee shop towards me. I looked up and smiled, but it was like he didn't see me. He was in his mid-thirties with short black hair and a neat black beard. He wore the blue shirt and pants of the crew, and I saw he had a name badge with 'Marek' on it. He went to the door, the same door that kept opening and closing like it was chewing something. I almost warned him to be careful, but he was a practical man, a working man. He would think me foolish.

I guessed there must be a sensor on it that told the ship's crew it kept opening. Marek went outside. I thought he'd need a coat, but he didn't have one. I couldn't see him so he must be checking from outside why the door kept coming open.

I finished my story. It was now 3 a.m. Time for another attempt at sleep. I got up, took off my reading glasses and returned to our cabin.

Sally had slept through it all. I smiled as I lay down on my bunk. How foolish I'd been to think of an old bulkhead door as a hungry mouth. Strange what imagination can do in the middle of the night.

The next day, we went for breakfast in the coffee area where I'd sat in in the depths of the night before. I chit-chatted to the woman serving the coffee as she poured frothy milk into the big mugs. 'It's a lot busier than it was in the middle of last night,' I said, by way of making conversation.

The woman turned to me, smiling. 'Last night? We were closed from seven.'

I laughed. 'I know. It was spooky being here on my own. Especially with that door opening.'

She frowned, pointed at the door. 'That one ? That door opened on its own?'

'Yes, hard to believe such a heavy door could open and shut like that. But they sent someone to fix it: one of the night crew.'

Her frown deepened. 'Night crew?'

'Yes, a man with a black beard. Called Marek—from his name-badge.'

She stepped back, went quiet.

It was my turn to frown. 'What is it?'

She couldn't meet my eye. She said, 'We don't have any crew members called Marek. But we did. About a year ago a steward called Marek jumped from Deck 7 into the North Sea. It would be this time of year. About 3 a.m.'

4

THE SNOW GLOBE

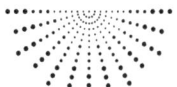

I was late getting away that year. I ran into Professor Ó Floinn in the echoey, empty central rooms of the Irish and Celtic Studies Department of Trinity College. 'James,' he said, 'I thought you'd be home by now.'

Ó Floinn was a tall man with a long face and big nose with black hair gone mostly grey. I was lucky enough to have him as supervisor to my PhD on Irish Monastic Settlements on the Cumbrian coast.

I grinned. 'Just finishing the chapter about Beckermet.' My enthusiasm spilled over. 'I think it's definite that the two surviving churches represent related but separate male and female monastic settlements with St John's being the male and St Bridget's female…'

'And you're convinced that the inscription in the churchyard is actually Old Irish?'

I nodded. 'I found a high-resolution scan of the stone in a book about medieval flooring of all places. But my Old Irish isn't the best.'

'Get Ó Murchu to look at it, he's your man for onomastics, but not now, obviously.'

I nodded wisely. 'No, not now. Too close to Christmas.'

Ó Floinn said, 'Don't stay here too long. I take it you're going back to England?' He asked.

'Just my mum left there, but my sister will be back from Manchester too.'

'Well, get away with you, and *Nollaig shona dhuit*. I'll see you in the New Year, then we'll take a look at that old PhD of yours.'

It was the twenty-second of December, and I was booked on the morning ferry the next day, but I still hadn't got mum everything I wanted to get her. I just had the intuition that something was missing, and so, I went from Trinity College straight to the Dublin Christmas Market.

The Christmas Market was packed with revellers eating bratwurst and chips and drinking Gluhwein and Guinness, sitting around at wooden tables, wrapped up in scarfs and hats against the biting easterly wind and laughing among a newly grown forest of fir trees.

There were stalls selling toffee and fudge and paella and wooden reindeers with Romanians, Poles, Irishmen and Welshmen all trying to sell you things you didn't need—that nobody needed but bought anyway because they sparkled and were brightly painted and reminded you why you loved Christmas with its lights and tinsel and laughing strangers.

Nothing much caught my eye for mum, until I saw a stall laden with antiques. A bunch of weird things all flung together: Japanese swords, Chinese and Dutch porcelain, two gilt Belgian Christs with Mary, a coronation plate for George V, some antique marbles, a framed proclamation of the Irish Republic in Gaelic and a snow globe. It was the snow globe that made me stop—the way the lights fell on it, and a kid had just shaken it up and walked off, so the cloud of tiny white snowflakes was still settling on a village scene of houses and trees and a little church. I picked it up. The glass ball and liquid inside made it heavy. 'How much is this?' I asked.

The proprietor, a thick-set Irishman with grey whiskers and a stomach barely contained within his waistcoat and heavy woollen overcoat raised a hand where fingers protruded from his fingerless gloves.

'That'll be thirty euros. It's an antique. Made in Kilkenny, 1950 or so.'

'1950 isn't an antique.'

'No, but pure vintage. It's a nice piece, you've got to admit.'

I shook the globe causing its snow to swirl in a miniature blizzard obscuring the church and village in a cloud of white that gently, slowly settled, pulling at my heart as it did so. It was nice but not worth thirty euros. As I turned it, I saw marks on the bottom of the wooden base. They looked like initials: DD.

I said, 'It's scratched.'

'No,' he shook his head. 'That's a previous owner's initials. It enhances the value. I should be asking forty.'

I put the globe down. I wasn't going to pay thirty euros. The initials didn't make it more valuable to me. Even though I'd placed it back on his table, I looked at the snow globe wistfully. The light from the surrounding stalls caught it and shone from its ball of glass. From behind, I caught a snatch of fairground music as the Merry-Go-Round with its painted dancing horses went round and round. But thirty euros was too much. 'Thanks,' I said.

I'd got ten paces when he called after me, 'I'll let you have it for twenty.'

And that was that. With a grin, I went back. 'Pleasure doing business with you,' I said as I handed him a twenty euro note. The truth was, I thought it was just the thing for my mother. She loved old things, and she loved Christmas. The snow globe was ideal.

Back in my draughty flat that afternoon, I did my packing. All my friends had gone home for the holidays, and the house I lived in was empty. I watched TV, but the night was cold and windy, and I thought I'd be better off under my duvet.

I fell asleep almost immediately and dreamt of my father. I used to dream about him a lot just after he died, but over the years it had got less. In the dream, he was young again, just like he was when I was a boy with his dark hair and the cigarette always in his fingers. That's what had killed him. That and all the fried breakfasts. Typical Irishman.

It wasn't a bad dream. We were talking about fishing, but I woke into the darkness. I felt strangely emotional. I still missed him.

The house was quiet inside but outside the east wind roared from over the Irish Sea. The roof shook and creaked, and the windows moaned as the air got in, cold drafts blowing under the door and then stopping only when the wind shifted, just to start again minutes later when it shifted back.

And then, in the middle of that dark night, there was light: golden sparkling light projected in a wandering circle, spinning around the ceiling and walls.

I sat up. I'd left the snow globe on the table by the door, and it was from this that the light came. Staring, I saw the snow dance within the globe as if someone had shaken it. There must be a light bulb in it. Maybe the wind had rocked the table and set it off? But it was lovely. I lay back and watched the golden lights move in a slow circle around the ceiling, shimmering as the tiny flecks of snow whirled inside the globe and cast their shadows against the shimmering veil of gold.

I thought of getting up to switch off the light so as not to waste the battery, but I didn't. I just lay there watching the dance of golden snow on my ceiling and walls. And then I slept again.

Once again, dad came into my dreams. He was trying to tell me something. He was speaking, but I couldn't make out a word.

I awoke late. I slept through my alarm, and I was in a panic. The light in the snow globe was off. Strangely, I couldn't find a switch to turn it on or off, but I needed to get to the ferry at Dún Laoghaire for my sailing. I had to be there an hour in advance. I could still do it, but it would be a close-run thing. I stuffed my wash-bag into my case and pushed the snow globe into the hold-all. I'd wrap it for mum when I got back home to Millom. At the door, I checked I had everything I needed but time was so short, so I'd gone to the extravagance of a taxi. He kept me waiting fifteen minutes before he pulled up outside in his blue Skoda. I was waiting for him with my bags.

'James Dempsey?' he said.

I nodded. 'That's me. Can we hurry?'

'For Dun Laoghaire?'

'Yes. The ferry. I'm getting the 12 pm one.'

'Okay, jump in. You're cutting it fine, and the traffic's evil today.'

'Can we still make it?'

'Sure, sure. Don't worry.'

Inevitably, as we idled in traffic, the taxi driver talked to me. 'English, are ye?' He said.

'My dad was Irish.' I always said that in Ireland as a defence. Relations between England and Ireland had not been happy down the centuries, and my father being Irish helped smooth things when things needed smoothing, which was only sometimes.

'Where from?'

'Eh?'

'Where in Ireland was your dad from?'

We were really late now. 'County Monaghan,' I said. 'But he worked in Dublin. At the prison.'

'Prison warder?'

'Yes.' I wished he'd just drive.

Then there was a movement in the traffic queue. Thank God.

He kept quiet as we drove closer to the ferry port, before stopping at lights. As we waited, minute after minute ticking by, he said, 'What ye doing here?'

'I'm a student at Trinity. Doing a PhD.'

'You came to Ireland though because of your dad?'

'Something like that.' We just needed to get moving.

'You should claim your Irish passport before that Brexit,' was his next piece of advice.

The traffic was really heavy with all the Christmas shoppers and people had taken their cars rather than walk anywhere because of the rain.

'Terrible weather last night,' he said.

I remembered the roaring wind. 'Yes. It was wild.' I looked at my watch.

'It'll be a rough crossing. I hope you've got your sick bag.' he said.

I wasn't generally sea-sick, but there had been dire warnings. I would be crossing to Liverpool and then getting the train to Millom where my mum lived.

We were still a mile or so short of Dún Laoghaire.

'It's the Christmas Market in Dún Laoghaire that's snarled it all up,' the taxi driver said.

Definite now. I was going to be late. I hoped they'd hold the boat.

And then all the electrics in the car died.

'Well, I'll be damned,' the driver said. 'Would you look at that! The car's just gone and died.'

I was sat jammed in the back. I had a suitcase and a hold-all up against me. A strange heat emanated from somewhere in it. I touched the bag and felt the glassy bulge of the Snow Globe through the fabric. It was glowing hot, and I could see the light through the material of the bag.

The driver got out. 'I'm going to have to call the breakdown,' he said. 'I don't understand it.'

'I'll miss my ferry!'

'I'm really sorry, mate. There's nothing I can do. I've never had this happen before, but it won't go.'

At least he had the grace not to charge me. I jumped out of the taxi. I had my case and my hold-all and a mile to go.

I was wheezing and out of breath when I got to the ferry port, and I still missed the ferry. It sailed without me.

What was worse was that the next ones were cancelled because of the weather. I thought about going back to my flat in Dublin, but then I'd just have to come back the next day and risk missing the boat again. I sighed and found somewhere to sit. I had some chips and beans to pass the time and a couple of pints of Guinness and fell asleep on an uncomfortable plastic chair in the ferry port lounge.

I AWOKE with a crick in my neck to the sound of my phone ringing. As I came to, reaching for the phone in my pocket, I saw nearly everyone in the ferry terminal hall was standing up staring at the TV screens that showed the 24-hour news broadcast. Some of the people in the waiting room had their hands to their faces, others were weeping openly. The news showed footage of dark stormy seas and lights. It was hard to make out what was happening. But someone was ringing me. I answered my phone.

'Are you all right?'

At first, I was so numbed with sleep that I didn't understand. I said, 'Mum?'

'Yes, James, me. I've been so worried. Where are you?'

'In the ferry terminal at Dún Laoghaire. I missed my boat. I forgot to text.'

'Thank God, Thank God.'

'What?' And then it all made sense. I said, 'I'm fine, mum. I'll ring you back,' and went to look at the screens.

The ferry boat *The Oisín* was sinking. Hundreds were dead, more were being winched off by Irish and British helicopter crews braving the storm. It wasn't clear what had happened. People said some freak wave had shipped tons of water into the ferry through the car deck door. No one really knew how it happened. Many speculated, but that didn't help the victims or their families.

One thing was sure. If I'd got to the port on time, I would be dead.

But still, people had to get places. It was Christmas—hundreds were travelling. They put on extra ferries. The weather had abated somewhat, but the mood was still sombre. Endless news broadcasts everywhere I went and the numbers of the dead jumping out from every newspaper hoarding I passed. I crossed the Irish Sea on Christmas Eve. From Liverpool, I took a train, changing twice before I got to Millom

The weather was not Christmassy, no snow, just clouds threatening rain over the familiar Lakeland fells. And people around me on the train or on the platforms talked of everyday things while I sat quietly. I was so preoccupied, I couldn't even read my book; I just kept thinking of my luck in surviving that disaster.

Mum picked me up at the station in her old Fiesta. I thought she'd never let me go, she hugged me so tight. My sister, Aisling, was there too. She kissed me and hugged me. They were both crying.

'I'm fine, I'm fine,' I said. 'Stop crying!'

Christmas Eve, finally home. Mum opened a bottle of wine. As we sat, she said, 'I wish your dad was here.'

I did too.

We were in the room of the old farmhouse with its blazing fire under the shadow of Black Combe. The room was warm, the Christmas Tree lights flashed, and the tinsel sparkled with the reflected light from the fire.

It was our tradition to open one gift on Christmas Eve so I got out the sketch pad and artists pencils I'd got in Dublin for Aisling. She unwrapped it and clearly loved the present. Then I got the heavy snow globe for mum. I'd wrapped it in metallic gold paper, just after I got home.

'What is it?' She shook the present mischievously, still without unwrapping it.

'You'll have to see,' I said.

'Unwrap it, mum!' Aisling laughed.

She unwrapped it quickly, ripping off the paper and then stopped with it only half-unwrapped, a strange look on her face. The light from the snow globe bathed her face in gold. The light must have switched itself on again. As she sat with it cupped in her two hands, the shimmering light shone round the walls and ceiling. It seemed twice as bright as it had been in my room in Dublin. I couldn't read the look on mum's face, but Aisling's was plain wonder.

Mum was frowning.

Aisling went quiet and glanced at me. I shrugged. 'Don't you like it, mum? It's nothing much. I just...'

When she looked at me, I saw she was crying.

I didn't get it. 'What?' I said, wondering. She turned the globe over and looked at its wooden base. She was still silent and wiped away her tears with the back of her hand.

'What?' I said again.

Aisling looked puzzled.

Mum tried to clear her throat to speak but couldn't.

I was anxious I'd upset her now, but I had no idea how.

Finally, she spoke. She said, 'Did you see the bottom?'

I said, 'Yes. The scratches—or initials.'

'DD.' She handed me the snow globe.

Yes, it could be DD.

'Dermot Dempsey,' she said.

'Dad?' Aisling said.

My mother nodded. 'It was his.'

I was almost dumbfounded. 'But how?' I told her I got it on a market stall in Dublin.

She said it was dad's as a boy in Ireland. She thought it had gone with his mother's things when they cleared the house in Monaghan. She had no idea where it went. But it had ended up on a stall in Dublin, and I'd picked it for her.

Later, my sister Aisling came to stand by me in the kitchen as I microwaved some Marks & Spencer's Sausage Rolls.

'Weird coincidence, eh?' she said, wine in hand.

I felt strange. I remembered the taxi breaking down. I remembered the light in my room in Dublin that woke me up, so I overslept.

Dermot Dempsey—my dad, looking after me still.

5

THE PATRON SAINT OF THIEVES

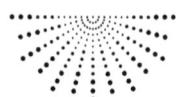

*V*enice, 23rd December, 6 pm, and a fine white snow sleeted down from a black wet sky, insinuating itself into the canals, into the alleys, and into the faces of those passers-by who stood and walked, amazed and enthralled by the visions and wonders old Venice could still conjure. Even after all those centuries, the City of Masks was always full of magic—magic and shadows.

Coloured Christmas lights strung over the bridges, twined between balconies of ancient buildings, sparkled in the chill air and reflected in the still waters of the narrow rios. These festive lights, reflections of a million hopes and a thousand wishes, skipped over the slight waves of the Grand Canal.

Christmas! An opportunity for relaxation, an opportunity for company, an opportunity for profit.

Alfonso the Snake wiped the snow from his eyes. At another time, snow in Venice was a marvel, but now, to him, it was an annoyance.

Alfonso was a thief, a handbag thief to be precise. But this particular night, sidelong to Christmas, work hadn't gone so well, and he was running late.

Handbag theft was a day job, but it was now night, and Alfonso was working late. As usual, he had left his present-buying to the last moment and didn't yet have enough cash to get the gifts he had set his heart on. He wanted gorgeous, generous things for his children and an elegant necklace for his beloved wife, Elena.

By day a thief, by night a devoted father. By this time, he should have been with his children already, so he had ground to cover.

The tree decorations glittered and the illuminations of the Christmas Market stalls spangled in the canal water as Alfonso hurried over the Accademia bridge, heading to St Mark's Square via the Fenice Theatre.

Someone offered him spiced wine, scented with nutmeg and cloves. It was free too. Another time, but now no time, so Alfonso sped on.

He took a few trifles along his way, pilfered lightly from unguarded pockets, but nothing really worth his while. He cut the bags by snipping their straps with a knife, honed razor-sharp, but chose his opportunities carefully, slicing off a finger-end would not do. People tended to raise the alarm once bloodied.

Alfonso preferred subtlety. His father had said that to him once when he was only ten, adding, 'You're a sly fox, Alfonso.' And his father being a police officer did not mean that as a compliment. Yes, Alfonso's father was a policeman. Funny how things turn out. Or not.

What was technically called wrong always attracted Alfonso with greater force than what might officially be called legal. Alfonso disputed those over-polarised, rather straight-jacketed criteria, but being an open-minded man, he was aware that others did not always agree with his freer understanding of the laws of property.

Mildly religious, Alfonso stepped into the tiny Church of St Dismas, dipped his fingers in the stoup, crossed himself and said a prayer to the patron saint of thieves. Again, a technicality suggested St Dismas was the patron saint of repentant thieves only, and Alfonso could not yet afford to be repentant. He had presents to buy.

He kneeled and crossed himself. Ahead the altar glimmered in the sacred gloom, crusted with semi-precious stones: quartz, calcite and chalcedony.

A bas relief of the crucifixion on Golgotha was hammered in silver on the wall behind the altar. On Christ's right was the penitent thief, St Dismas. On Christ's left was the impious thief who challenged Jesus to save them all if he was indeed the Messiah. We know Dimas's name, but the impenitent thief is forgotten, his name lost in history and his soul lost in hell. Think on that as a lesson, if you will: don't argue with your spiritual betters.

Alfonso took a moment and took in the vestments and sculptures. A statue of the virgin stood on the sinister side, her forgiving son on the dexter, glittering gold in the candlelight. The air burned fragrant with incense and old wood.

Alfonso turned and the priest, who had slipped quietly up behind him, taking him for a punter, recognised our thief and exhaled.

Alfonso stopped, a brief exchange of glances ensued. In the end, the priest lowered his gaze and muttered, 'Are you here for your confession, Alfonso?'

'Not yet, Father, but soon.' Alfonso gave a rakish smile, exited and, outside the church, looked back. Regrets flooded him like soft, sweet candyfloss: melancholy was our man's favourite mood.

"One day," Alfonso whispered. "I will repent. But for now, I have a family to feed."

That sharpened him. The air was cold. He longed to be back home with his wife and two little daughters and their cousin Simone. And it grew late, but first, just one fish, just one big fish, hauled out of the sea of lady shoppers, was all he needed. With one little success he would feed the five thousand, or at least the five who would be at his house when he got back.

Venice is full of narrow alleys, and it is easy for those who do not know their way to get lost, very lost, almost irredeemably lost. But Alfonso, he didn't get lost. Alfonso knew his way.

The thief darted from alley to alley, down the quick-routes and the short-cuts, but then something startled him, and he stopped short.

Alfonso's heart fluttered. His eyes disbelieved their seeing. Someone—someone giving off light like Christmas itself—crossed his route at the end of the narrow way.

It seemed to Alfonso that he could see the dirty wall through this flitting figure, this luminescent figure, this figure you could see through.

What was this? A ghost? Surely these Venetian streets had seen enough death to raise a multitude of revenants, but there was something about this man that was not ghostlike at all. He was supernatural perhaps, but not simply a spectre.

Alfonso held his throat and stared. He was no believer in wraiths. In fact, he scoffed at the weak-minded who gave credence to such things. He shook his head and blinked and then the glowing, cowled man was gone.

Standing, getting damp, Alfonso shrugged. There must be an explanation for this that would stand in the light of day. It must all be because of the good gorgonzola he ate for lunch. That, taken with the Aperol Spritz he had guzzled, would account for it.

Alfonso certainly wasn't going to start believing in spirits now. He clicked his tongue as if to chide his unreliable eyes and hurried on.

The snow continued to fall, but fall without sticking. It simply dissolved where it lay. Still it drifted down like a soft, wet, flitter-float of falling swan's down.

St Mark's Square had a beautiful Christmas Tree down towards the Doge's Palace side, opposite San Marco's Cathedral. The tree was modern-looking with a shining angel on top, lights on the branches twinkling, and thin tinsel streamers in gold, fluttering in the slight breeze, sparkling among the electric stars clustered on the tree's golden branches.

The air here was warmer and the snowflakes fewer. The crowd smelled of eau de cologne and coffee. A band played Italian favourites while tourists thronged the area between the colonnades and occupied the cafe tables, wrapped up in hats and scarves and gloves against the December weather.

These were prime hunting waters for Alfonso the Shark, but there were carabinieri here who knew him. He saw one tip another off of his arrival. The Shark would not be fishing here tonight.

Alfonso grunted, then slipped up into the narrow, twisting alleys of the Merceria. This was better.

Glittering shops with watches and jewellery, shining ceramics and display lights turned up bright to show off the wares in the windows.

Precious things were laid out—strings of pearls, blue sapphire earrings, bracelets and rings: rings that sparkled as if they were on fire, catching hints of red and blue and yellow in the diamonds, and opals with hearts of coloured flame that only opened to the eyes of those who lingered to look. And many did.

Bright glass windows showing off gleaming catches on fine red handbags, leather goods galore. The smell of tanned leather was strong, and mixed with the aromas of wine and cigars and pizza and well-dressed, perfumed people

There were people everywhere, pressed in tight on all sides: perfect.

Alfonso palmed his razor-knife from where it usually rested up his sleeve. It was thin and sharp—so sharp you could shave with it—and with a practised move, he flicked it until it lurked like a fang, cradled carefully between his fingers.

He saw his victim and moved so quickly and pleasantly that no one noticed what he did. He sliced and clicked and took. The woman was preoccupied with her man friend and, from the way she grinned at him, you would think he was Brad Pitt or Marlon Brando. Brando at least had the merit of being Italian.

Anyway, this guy was effete, a foreigner, though Alfonso would not stay to fight, he would be off, light-toed, down sinuous alleys and passageways drenched in darkness before any trouble caught him.

But they did not even notice, so entranced they were with each other and the lights and the conviviality, and probably an Aperol Spritz or two. Maybe a Campari.

And they weren't married. No ring. Alfonso saw that. Not even engaged.

Back in the alley, Alfonso checked out the bag. There was little in there. The careful woman must have kept her credit cards elsewhere, and though he found a scrunched ten euros at the bottom of the bag, it was not enough. Alfonso sniffed, dropped the purse and re-entered the fray.

Ahead, a crowd of tourists shoaled like so many innocent fishes—Dutch, German, maybe English. Blondes, anyway: red-faced. All those northerners looked the same, but then he heard it: definitely English with its 'chs' and 'shs' and 't-t-t'.

Perhaps they were off a cruise ship or even staying over a few days in Venice.

Still, they had that awkward familiarity of the tour group, people thrown together temporarily, making the best of it, but hoping for the company soon to end, so they could escape from their newfound friends. Then they would return with a sour satisfaction to the familiar miseries of their unhappy lives.

Alfonso glanced discreetly. He was a sniffer-dog. He'd done this business so long it was second nature to him to pick a pocket, to choose a victim, to set a mark.

He saw two, an older woman, late seventies and maybe her grand-daughter—a young lass of perhaps twenty-five. The pair perused a book shop that sold antique volumes designed never to be read, just to look nice on the shelves and add an air of learning to someone's suburban home.

The two ladies nodded, muttered words of appreciation or of dislike, then moved on to the next shop.

Not for the first time, Alfonso mused that all the stores in this part of Venice sold the same things; there was a leather shop, a jewellery shop, a fancy stationer, a shop selling masks, a shop selling Murano glass, then mix up and repeat.

The two target women ambled behind their group. The older had a handbag, and she wasn't paying attention. The younger wanted to be elsewhere; she kept checking they weren't getting separated from the group with edgy looks cast ahead while her grandmother dawdled.

Yes, a lovely red handbag, the grandmother had, held in loose fingers, straps showing a good few centimetres that would be easy to cut.

And now was the time.

Alfonso swooped like an eagle, coming in undetected. The grandmother didn't even turn her head, didn't flinch, didn't notice as he severed her straps and relieved her of the handbag's weight.

Alfonso stepped right, then back, then into a doorway, and turned off and up a narrow alley so dark and dismal, not one tourist would venture after him.

For the victim, a theft is a monstrous grievance, but for the thief it's merely graft. And now, thought Alfonso, not even a grievance because neither the old dear nor her granddaughter had noticed.

He slipped into shadows, moving like a cat on a cloudy night, like an octopus vanishing into ink. Then he stopped and stood under a streetlight so he could see his prize.

It was amazing how much distance he could cover in an eyeblink, but then he had much practice. Alfonso's nose sniffed. It was still snowing. He rifled the contents of the red handbag, and there in the bottom was a bracelet.

He stopped. His fingers hovered. Could it be as nice as it looked?

The bracelet glittered and gleamed even more brightly as he turned it in the light the streetlamp shed. He marvelled at the hard, pointed jewels and fingered the smooth, cool gold, twisting it around in his fingers. The bracelet was big and heavy, and it spangled under a seedy Venetian alley light.

"Wow!" he said. Alfonso was no jeweller, but to him, this looked to be worth a ton.

Alfonso lifted his head to heaven and thanked St Dismas for his patronage. Christmas in Alfonso's humble house was going to be special this year.

He dropped the red leather bag without a thought and stuffed the bracelet into his jacket pocket.

With a happy heart, Alfonso almost skipped down the alley. No need for him to risk more jobs tonight. He would treat himself to a bottle of Aperol to celebrate when he got home.

Feeling like all his dreams had come true, he dashed at a run over the Rialto Bridge, but then stopped with a skid to look down the Grand Canal. The crowds of merrymakers lifted his heart. He hoped that all those people would have the most beautiful Christmas. Just like him.

Oh, how he loved Venice! And oh, how he loved this night! The Grand Canal smelled of moonlight and mystery. The dreams of a million lovers drifted along its bobbing waves like roses on the Ganges, like Chinese Lanterns rising in a winter sky.

Coloured Christmas lights from the palazzos that lined the canal rippled like diamonds, emeralds or sapphires and glittered on the water like a broken necklace, all the stones gone scattered and hiding in alcoves and shadowed corners until the dark canal doused their light, a light that was reborn with the next pulse of electricity through the midwinter wires.

Snow kissed his cheek, but this time he found its caress was lovely. "Belissimo! Belissimo!" he yelled at the clouds, causing passers-by to look and grin at his merriment, joining in with his mirth and wishing him a Merry Christmas.

He wished it back.

Coming down off the bridge then into a maze of streets, a left, a right, a left and several more twists and then he stopped at a corner shop off a campo where he was well known.

"You're in a good mood," the shopkeeper said, flicking the ash from her cigarette into a cup.

He bought a bottle of Aperol and some tiramisu as a treat.

"Oh, yes, Chiara, my dear. What a lovely night it is. Merry Christmas by the way, I hope you and your family have a lovely time."

The shopkeeper laughed. "Thanks, Alfonso. You too. Give my regards to Elena and the kids."

Everyone knew Alfonso was a thief, but he was funny, and he didn't steal from them, only tourists, so they didn't mind.

Alfonso couldn't get over how beautiful the night was, what with the lights and the snow and everyone happy and on holiday. He crossed the campo with its church, and strings of Christmas stars reflecting on the water of the little rio that ran to the left.

A more expansive stretch of water confronted him: the Rio di San Lorenzo. A bridge arched over the water to his right, but Alfonso was so bright-hearted with his stolen prize that he glanced at the moored boats, and grinned: that would make an alternative bridge.

Not as safe as the other, but he was enjoying a streak of luck. Born lucky. Favoured by saints and angels.

He got to the edge, laughed out loud, then leapt. The boat rocked as he landed. He laughed and jumped again and, having jumped, plunged from boat to boat, until he was over the canal and tip-toed, almost over-balanced, onto the lip of dry land and into the Campo di San Lorenzo.

And then, in front of him flashed the apparition. The same ethereal figure he'd seen at the end of the alley earlier. The glowing thing loomed up, and Alfonso fell back.

Alfonso toppled into the dirty canal water. Once it had been the home of dolphins, now it was a rats' highway, smelling of diesel from the countless small boats, drifting not with lovers' dreams but with orange peel and plastic water bottles. Sometimes condoms.

Damn those tourists who came in their millions to admire Venice and then polluted it without a second thought.

Alfonso swam; Alfonso splashed; Alfonso went under. His foot tangled in the mooring rope that lurked underwater. He snagged, and couldn't get free.

Bubbles ruptured from his mouth in a dark trail up to the surface. He felt his lungs tighten. Every scrabbling movement, every fumbled twist of his fingers sucked his oxygen.

His heart burned. He longed to breathe, but breathing was drowning, and he couldn't afford to do that. He forced himself to focus and untie his foot. His shoe came off and floated up. The rope had him. The rope was killing him. He would drown just inches from the air.

Images of his children flashed before his eyes, a procession of memories and imagined futures. His wife Elena grinned and beckoned him to bed. He saw his mother smiling and his father frowning, and then Alfonso's consciousness blurred and filled with canal water, dark and druglike and deadly.

The glowing visitation appeared around him, and all was suddenly bright. He saw the dirty bottom of the canal with its stones and slimy coins and animal bones all lit up. The stone embankments and the bottoms of boats were visible with a nest of trailing ropes—the ropes that had him tight.

The ghost spoke. Its voice entered his ear and slid through his mind. It said, "What you have done, I forgive; what you will do, I commend. What you fail to do, I will punish".

"Please", he said, silver bubbles trailing from his mouth, catching the ghostly light like mini moons and pearls. "I have a wife and children. Please, don't let me die. I am a mother's son, as I guess you once were. If you have any mercy, don't let me die!"

The ghost looked on, and he saw it had the same face as the painted St Dismas in the little church.

"Mercy?" The ghost said. "What do you know of mercy?"

"Let me live, and I promise I'll change. I will repent."

"I'll hold you to that," St Dismas said.

One last time, Alfonso twisted the rope around his ankle and pushed and he was free. He broke the surface and gasped for air, and then he realised the bracelet had fallen from his pocket.

The glowing figure stood now on the embankment, but its light suffused the water and all around. With a sigh, Alfonso dived for the bracelet. He found it at the bottom of the canal, snatched it up and swam.

No longer at risk of drowning, he dragged himself up onto the parapet, and lay in a puddle that reflected the Campo's Christmas Tree lights.

And there still stood the ghost. Alfonso's blood froze. He backed off, almost going in again. His heart hammered and water dripped from him. The spirit of the dead thief stood above and raised a warning finger.

Alfonso's hand gripped the bracelet hard. He stuffed it into the pocket of his sopping wet jacket. The ghost of St Dismas wanted him to give it back, he knew that, but to give it back! That would mean no presents for his kids, no present for Elena.

The old woman could afford it. She was a rich tourist. She probably had six of them at home, and anyway it would be insured. It was a victimless crime, hell, it wasn't even a crime, really.

Alfonso stared at the ghost. His heart quailed, but he would not give in. He would be steadfast. He only stole for good reasons, for the best reasons, simply to look after those he loved, and—himself—a little.

He was about to say as much to the glowering spirit when it was gone. It vanished like smoke from the February fireworks of the Carnivale.

Alfonso stood up, dripped and shivered. It was December, after all. The snow had stopped for now, but it was still freezing. Luckily he didn't live too far from here, just off the Campo di Pozzi. He started off at a run, and every few steps patted his jacket to make sure the diamond bracelet was still secure. Damn Dismas! He wouldn't give it back. This was the ticket to the good life his family deserved. Hell, that *he* deserved.

And then, as he came round a corner, he saw his wife, Elena. This was not a total surprise. Elena worked in a small hotel here, but she was late finishing. As he watched her, he thought about how lucky he was. She was a beautiful, soft-eyed woman, as lovely and beloved to him as when he first met her when they were sixteen.

Alfonso squeezed the stolen bracelet and thought of what he would buy for her once he had fenced it. Or maybe he'd give her the bracelet and watch it glitter on her beautiful wrist when he took her out for a first-class meal at Sammy's. Alfonso scratched his head. But then, what would he give his daughters? No, he would have to sell the bracelet and buy them all something with the proceeds. All that was fine. But he couldn't give it back.

He was about to step out and shout, 'Boo!" when he saw she was not alone. Elena stood at the door, talking to some foreigners, English babbling from their lips.

Alfonso took a pace right to see better, and to his astonishment and horror, he saw they were the grandmother and granddaughter, the ones he had stolen the bracelet from. How could this be? What strange parable was unfolding here two nights before Christmas?

He tried to calm himself. No, it was just a coincidence, nothing to do with the patron saint of thieves.

But it was those very two. Alfonso stood and shivered, and not just from cold. Then Elena saw him and frowned. She smiled and nodded to the two English women. Alfonso saw the older woman was in tears.

Elena said goodbye, and the two tourists entered the hotel, the younger consoling the older with an arm around her shoulder.

Elena came close to kiss him, then pulled back. "How come you're so wet?"

"Who are those two?"

"Tourists staying at the hotel. But why are you so wet?"

Alfonso stuttered. "W-why was the old one crying?"

Elena shrugged. "Someone stole her handbag. It had an heirloom in it."

"An heirloom?"

"Belonged to her grandmother."

"The old one's grandmother?' He stroked his chin. "It must be really old then." That was good.

Elena said, "What do you care? But why are you so wet?"

"I fell in the canal."

Elena burst out laughing. She couldn't speak because of the sobs of laughter that wracked her. She even had to lean against the wall for support.

Alfonso scowled. "It's not funny. Come on, let's go home. I'm freezing."

He went to link arms with her but she instantly recoiled. "No, you're drenched."

Alfonso's mind was on the stolen bracelet, indeed the stolen bracelet suffused all his thoughts. There wasn't even room for a thought about Aperol Spritz or betting on the horses.

If the bracelet was old, the grandmother's grandmother's bracelet, and kept so long in the family, it must be worth a fortune. Behind his dreams of avarice, one quiet image of an old woman in tears presented itself. He exhaled and thrust that picture away.

Seeking to keep thoughts of the old woman out of his head, he asked, "What's for dinner?".

"You tell me," Elena said. "You're cooking it."

In the house, he stuffed the stolen bracelet in the drawer in the bedroom chest, under his socks, after once gazing at it and sighing.

No sooner did they get home than he changed into to dry clothes. In the living room, he greeted his family and was hugged in return. Then a virtuoso improvisation and Alfonso ushered his two daughters, their cousin, and Elena to a plate of Sicilian Caponata.

"It's good, papa," the little one, Aurora, said.

Alfonso smiled. He was an intuitive and enthusiastic chef. Elena worked long hours at the hotel, but the hours of a handbag thief were much less regular, so he had time to study cooking. His own grandmother was Sicilian, and he had learned the spicy recipes of that island from her.

Also at dinner was the babysitter of his two daughters, who was also their cousin. He fed them all. And with laughter and wine for Alfonso and Elena and for Simone, the babysitter, as she was now fifteen, they laughed and joked among the Christmas decorations.

At the table, Elena said, "It was sad about that old lady."

"What old lady?" Simone asked, raising the glass to her lips. Elena told her the tale.

Simone glanced at Alfonso who frowned deeply. He didn't want to talk about some sad old woman, so he asked his daughters how their day had been and listened to their excitement about what they would be getting for Christmas.

Tomorrow was Christmas Eve, the day for Christmas shopping. He listened to his girls and thought how he would get up early and fence the bracelet and be back in time to buy them toys and sweets and clothes, and pretty shiny things they'd love. Maybe even a puppy. They'd love a puppy.

He turned back to Elena to hear her say, "And the worst thing is, the old one, the grandmother is dying. She has heart failure."

Simone said, "Oh, that's so sad."

Alfonso said, "Why did she come to Venice if she's dying?"

Elena frowned. "She's never been here before. The family is quite poor."

"Poor? Then how come she had a valuable bracelet?"

Elena's eyes narrowed. "I didn't say bracelet, I said heirloom. How did you know it was a bracelet?"

Alfonso shrugged. "I don't know. Guessed."

Elena gave him a shrewd look but said nothing.

Alfonso went on. "But I don't believe they're poor. The heirloom—

"

"—bracelet."

"Bracelet. It'll be insured."

"Apparently not. That's why she's so upset."

He sniffed. "Then it's her own fault. People should insure valuable things."

Elena and Simone both glared at him. Simone said, "Uncle Alfonso, that's a very cold and cruel thing to say."

Alfonso shrugged but couldn't meet her eyes. There was an awkward silence, and in the end, he said, "Anyone want any tiramisu? I bought some earlier."

"Bought?" Simone giggled, the wine gone to her head.

"Simone!" Elena said sharply, and Simone stifled her giggle.

LATER THAT NIGHT, Alfonso dreamed of St Dismas.

The saint said nothing, just glowed in his corner, staring at Alfonso, who still saw him through his closed eyelids. Give it back? What would he use to treat his family then? Fairydust?

He muttered, "No, Dismas. I will stand firm."

Minutes went by. Then he thought he heard the saint say, "Honesty begins with yourself. It is not too late, though it soon will be."

Through clenched teeth, Alfonso said, "No, Dismas. I will stand firm."

Alfonso lay awake for a long time, but he must have slept because when he awoke, St Dimas was gone.

· · ·

ELENA WAS ON AN EARLY SHIFT, so she was gone before he got up. In the early morning darkness, Alfonso got out of bed.

With a heavy heart, Alfonso went to the drawer where he'd hidden the bracelet. It was still there under his socks. By the yellow electric light, he examined the glittering thing. How beautiful it was, and old too, a proper antique. He sighed and rubbed his brow.

He thought of the old woman in tears at the loss of her bracelet.

He had to give it back. He hadn't thought he had a conscience, but it turned out he did. He would go to the hotel, give it back saying he'd found the handbag floating in the canal, and then he'd go Christmas shopping for his family. He didn't have much, but they'd have whatever he could afford.

First, he'd go to the hotel. Simone had gone home the previous night so he made breakfast for Aurora and Maria and they ate it watching television. Their mother didn't let them watch TV when they were eating their breakfast, so it was a treat when they were alone with daddy. They all three kept it secret because they didn't want to get busted.

After breakfast, he took the girls to the hotel. It had started to snow again, and the girls ran around trying to catch snowflakes on their tongues.

He rang the buzzer of the hotel. The staff of the hotel were so few, it was no surprise when Elena answered the door. She said, "What are you doing here?"

"I've come to see those two English ladies. The ones you were talking about last night."

She narrowed her eyes. "Them? Why?"

"It doesn't matter. Can you just tell me the room number?" He turned to his daughters. "Girls, you stay here with your mama. Which number, Elena?" He patted his jacket to feel the bracelet was still there.

"Six, but you can't go up."

Before she could say anything else, he was past her. "I won't be long."

"Alfonso!" But before Elena could explain further, Alfonso was up the stairs. There was no lift in this tiny hotel.

Walking along the corridor, he bumped into a doctor, and more ominously a priest.

They looked very sombre, but let him past as they went downstairs and out of the hotel.

Alfonso got to the door of Room Six and knocked. His English was reasonable, but he practised what he was going to say. He had the bracelet in his hand. He shuffled from foot to foot, gripping the thing. He rapped again. This was crazy. What was he going to do? He'd worked himself up to give it back, and now there was no one in.

He was about to turn when he heard a muffled. "Hang on. Scusi."

The door opened a crack. It was the granddaughter as it turned out.

Alfonso put on a big smile. "Signorina," he said.

She looked puzzled, frowned. She'd been crying. Her eyes were red and her mascara smudged. She looked at him suspiciously. He was holding the bracelet tightly between both hands. She probably thought he was trying to sell her something.

She muttered, "Now isn't a good time."

"Please," Alfonso said. He grew suddenly nervous that she wouldn't take the bracelet off him, and he would be left with his sin. He thrust the bracelet forward. "This is for you. It is yours."

The woman glanced down at the bracelet. "Grandma's bracelet! It was stolen yesterday."

Alfonso nodded gravely. "Yes, I found it in the canal. In a handbag."

She looked like she didn't believe him. "In the canal?"

"Yes, the handbag was ruined. I threw it away." He forced a smile. "But I have this for you. You say it's your grandmother's bracelet. Can I give it to her?"

Tears burst from the young woman's eyes and rolled down her cheeks. She thrust the back of her hand to her mouth and could not speak.

"Please take it. I found it. It is yours."

The woman broke down as sobs wracked her.

Alfonso began to think that something was terribly wrong. "What is the matter?"

"How did you track us down?" the woman said.

"My wife, she works here." Alfonso knew that did not really explain it, but the woman nodded anyway.

He said, "The bracelet is valuable, I think?"

The young woman laughed.

Why was she laughing?

He said, "It is old and full of diamonds. An heirloom?"

She dried her eyes with the back of her hand, smearing makeup down it. She said, "I'm afraid there won't be much of a reward for that."

Alfonso shook his head earnestly. The thought of a reward caught hold of him for a second, then he dismissed it. He would do the right thing for its own sake, not the wrong thing dressed up with lies designed to make him feel better about what he did.

The young woman's strange mirth unnerved him.

He frowned. "It is not valuable?"

"I'm afraid not."

How could that be? He gazed at the bracelet. "No? But it is old. And look at how many jewels?" The bracelet sparkled in the artificial light.

The woman laughed. "No, Grandma had dementia. It's just costume jewellery. She knew that once, but as she got confused about things, she began to call it her 'heirloom'."

Alfonso's face fell. "It is worthless?"

"More or less."

Alfonso said, "I don't want to keep it. Can I give it back to her, anyway?"

The woman took the bracelet from Alfonso's open hand. "No, I'll take it back. It'll remind me of her."

Alfonso looked past the woman, into the room she shared with her grandmother. He listened to the silence that rang heavy as a bell from within.

A doctor and a priest.

He gave the woman the bracelet, nodded and backed off.

Downstairs, Elena said, "You shouldn't have gone up there."

Alfonso didn't say anything.

Elena continued. "The old one died last night. Her heart went, perfectly natural causes., but at least she saw Venice before she died."

Alfonso remained silent and put his hand over his eyes.

Elena continued. "I would have told you, but you just leapt up those stairs."

He shook his head.

"What did you want to see them for anyway?"

Alfonso reached down and took the hands of his daughters. Elena followed him to the door, waving goodbye to the manager.

"Let's go Christmas shopping,' Alfonso said.

"I want a puppy,' Aurora, the youngest of his daughters, said.

"And I want a kitten," said Maria, the eldest.

Alfonso borrowed a gondola from a friend. He promised to bring it back, but he took his family down the Grand Canal on their way to do the last-minute Christmas shopping. The gondola skipped, slapped, slopped over the waves of the Grand Canal, Alfonso at its end, punting, his daughters gazing at the snow, and Elena smiling at her husband.

They had a happy Christmas, Alfonso with his wife and children, and they saw Elena's brother and on St Stephen's Day his own mother and father.

On January 2nd, Alfonso got a job. He started work as a sous-chef at Sammy's his favourite restaurant and taught them how to make Sicilian food like his grandmother.

Then he went to back to the Church of St Dismas.

"You won," he said. "And thanks."

It's hard to tell if a painted face is smiling.

6

MUSIC FROM ANOTHER ROOM

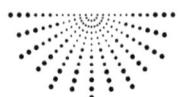

*D*ecember 19, 1977, Sighisoara, Romania, and I was lucky to arrive at all in that battered Dacia, what with the weather.

I ploughed through sprawling drifts of snow to enter the medieval city by the Clocktower Gate. The fourteenth-century tower watched over me as I came into the cobbled square. Everything was closed, shops battened up, houses shut. Street lights, far sparser than in the prosperous West, huddled in corners their yellow glare kindling the spinning snow.

I had a place to stay booked: the *Pension am Schneiderturm*. This was a German town once, but there were few Germans left in Sighisoara now.

I was booked in, but the trouble was that I couldn't find the place. The streets were narrow and difficult to drive along in the low light and worsening weather. God alone knew what was under the snow— holes or bricks. I would probably break an axle if I drove on.

I decided to park in the main square and make my way to my accommodation on foot. I left the car in a corner of the Clocktower Square and watched the snow begin to bury it.

From the boot, I took the suitcase that held everything I needed: clothes, flashlight, pencil, pen, paper, notebooks, portable typewriter, and a spare half-bottle of whisky I'd got in Belgrade, just in case I needed something to help me sleep.

As I shoved the car door shut, a peal of bells rang from the clock-tower high above, ghostly music for a deserted scene. The ringing melody sounded familiar, but I wondered whether I remembered it or merely imagined I did.

Fatigue fuddled my senses. All I wanted now after my drive through the Carpathian Mountains was something to eat and a warm bed. Well, that wasn't all I wanted, but I would be satisfied with those small comforts for now.

I glanced around the deserted space. If this square were in the West, it would be full of tourist shops and cafes, but there was nothing like that, just dour Communist emptiness. In a corner stood a tourist information office so shabby that it looked like they didn't want any tourists to come calling. The office was closed anyhow.

It was only 9 pm, but there were no bars visible, nor restaurants, just darkness speckled with the falling snow and a low blanket of cloud. It oppressed my spirit as well as froze my skin. I hurried off along the narrow streets, harried by snow that got in my mouth, eyes and soaked down the collar of my coat.

I had no hat. I wished I'd got a hat. I had gloves and a scarf but no hat. My shoes were also wet, and ice-water seeped into my socks.

After five minutes, I stopped, disorientated. Where the hell was I actually going? I consulted the hand-drawn map the guy at the tourist office in Brasov had given me and watched as it melted in the wet.

I stood under a street lamp in order to quickly read what still remained visible on the sodden paper. It seemed the *Pension Am Schneiderturm* was up ahead, left, right, then on a short way. It was a tower built into the city's encircling walls.

I shuffled through the snow, little heaps melting on the toes of my shoes, leaching in. With ice-cold, squelching feet, I crunched on through new snow.

The tips of nearby metal railings poked through a snow drift on a windswept street corner, stark black against the white, looking like crotchets and quavers on a music score.

And then I sighed. This way wasn't the right way. I retraced my steps, still visible in the snow-covered ground, turned left, but came to another dead end within minutes.

I gazed around the blank street. All the windows were shuttered, the doors locked. The houses frowned at me. Whatever life was inside was closed away, and I was alone with Sighisoara. I wondered if she remembered me.

At one point, I heard the tinkling of a piano. It must be coming from a house, but I couldn't tell which. At least something was alive in these streets.

Going round and up and down the snow-filled streets, I began to get a little freaked. The only person I'd seen since arriving was a hatted and gloved figure who'd hurried away before I could ask directions: some old man with more important business than helping a stranger find his way.

The blizzard blew feathers of snow in my eyes. The chill was getting to me. At one point, I even thought I heard a woman's voice muttering under the wind. She was speaking a language I knew I knew but couldn't place it: French, English, German maybe? But her words made no sense.

The long drive on icy roads, which even in good weather were terrible, crazily driven cars and suddenly coming on horses and traps with no lights and having to brake and swerve and slide on the snow had strained me. I was now imagining voices in the wind. I listened hard—voices and sometimes music.

If I couldn't find the pension, I'd settle for sleeping in the car now I thought. The cold outside was deathly. I exhaled, turned and walked, span round, trudged on, faced byways that went nowhere but finally found the Clocktower Square.

There was my car, half-buried. I regretted my unspoken words. Sleeping in the car wasn't appealing now I'd found it.

There was a woman. "Hello!" I shouted across, snowflakes on my tongue. I spat them out.

She looked like she was going to walk on, but I called again. Now she halted, hesitated and turned but didn't approach.

I walked closer, waving the wet rag that had been my map. "I'm looking for the Pension am Schneiderturm. I'm a tourist."

She shrugged and shook her head. I'd been optimistic to think she'd understand English. Hesitantly, I said the same thing in Romanian. I'd not wanted to speak Romanian.

Instead of looking pleased that I was speaking her language, she frowned.

I went on anyway. "Yes, I'm booked there tonight. I just wondered if you could direct me."

Her brow furrowed even more deeply. "You don't know?"

"No, I don't know Sighisoara. As I said, I'm a tourist."

"A tourist?"

This was getting tedious. "Yes. I can't find my way."

"Where are you from?"

I shrugged and wiped snowflakes out of my eyes with the back of my leather-gloved hand. "London, why?"

"England?"

I nodded rapidly. I understood they weren't used to tourists, but her reaction was strange.

In the end, she pointed and gave me directions. After I thanked her and was about to walk off, she apologised. "Sorry, I thought you were local."

"Ah, my Romanian?"

"Yes."

That was unfortunate, just what I'd hoped to avoid. I forced a laugh. "I had a good teacher back in London."

She said, "You sound like one of us."

"I'm not," I replied firmly. I nodded my thanks and left, ploughing down the narrow street she had indicated. I couldn't let that happen again. I'd have to be more careful in future.

Finally, I found the Pension am Schneiderturm. The city walls were dressed with inch-thick snow, and more blew around where I was to stay: the Tailors' Tower. Lights gleamed in welcome through the narrow latticed windows of the pension, beacons of orange light spilling out into the winter that whirled around the city. The snow, now lit, looked welcoming: Christmassy even.

I knocked on the heavy wooden door, and within minutes a slim, dark-haired man of around forty opened it. He smiled to see me. "Mr Roth, is it? We were expecting you earlier."

I nodded, wiping the wet from my face, blinking snowflakes off my eyelashes.

He smiled. "I'm Bodgan Tatarescu. I run the pension." He shook his head. "My, my, you look like a snowman!"

His English was excellent, that's why he probably got the job of running the pension. He was almost certainly an informer for the secret police. It didn't make him a bad man. That's how things were in Communist Romania.

He took my suitcase out of my hand to help me as I took off my coat and extracted my fingers from the sodden gloves. Snow fell off me in melting clumps onto the rug at the entrance.

Inside the Schneiderturm, I was struck by the age of the place. It was stone-built with gnarled wooden beams. Aged tapestries hung on the walls. My interest must have been apparent on my cold face.

"You like it?" Bogdan said, beaming.

"It's great. How old is it?" I stood, dripping, shuddering with the cold. Then the numbing hypothermia eased and blood returned to my hands and feet.

He said, "I'll give you the history. Come through into the main room. We have a fire, and I will fetch you wine. You prefer red or white?"

"Red please."

"Good, good. Good Romanian wine, nice and red like Dracula's blood! You like *Dracula*, right?"

I grinned and took off my shoes, but my wet socks squelched on the stone floor. He didn't seem to mind.

Bogdan hung my coat on a black hook on the wall, next to others. Then he showed me through to a room with a massive fireplace. Logs burned warmly. The smell took me back to campfires long past. The warm air toasted my cheeks and fluttered the topmost star on the small Christmas tree that stood in the corner. Little silver and gold baubles hung from its tinsel branches.

That must be for me, I thought. This guy Bogdan would either be a good Communist, and that was most likely given the role they'd awarded him, or he was Orthodox, and the Orthodox Christmas wasn't till later in the month. Still, it was a nice touch.

I sat in a comfortable chair, glad of the fire's warmth. My trousers started to steam.

Bogdan came back with a glass of red wine and handed it to me. With him this time was a woman he introduced as his wife, Diana. She was tall and brunette with the most striking-dark eyes and olive skin. It seemed she didn't speak much English, but I didn't make the mistake of talking Romanian this time. I nodded and smiled like people do the world over to indicate good-will.

They sat on the sofa opposite.

"So," Bogdan said. "It's nice to welcome you to the Schneiderturm. You would like to hear something of its history?"

I nodded and sipped my wine. I was starting to relax but knew that was dangerous. I would refuse a second glass.

Bogdan talked. "Sighisoara was a fortification of the Ancient Dacians, enemies of Rome."

I smiled politely, and he went on down the centuries. When he got to the Middle Ages, he said, "In the eleventh century, the King of Hungary, who ruled this area, invited Germans to settle here to defend him from the armies of the Turks. The Germans, they were specifically Saxons, owned this city for many centuries."

"*Schäsbrich,*" I said.

He looked at me thoughtfully. "In correct German, *Schäßburg.* The name you used is the slang of the Saxons."

Another mistake. The wine was loosening me too much. I put the half-full glass on the wooden side table.

"So, the Saxons arranged that each guild—you are familiar with the medieval guilds: butchers; tailors; stonemasons?"

"I'm familiar with the idea."

He nodded and smiled like a schoolteacher then went on. "Each

59

guild was given an area of the wall to defend, and each guild built a tower. This was the Tailor's Tower, the Schneiderturm."

"How long ago was that?" I asked

Bogdan said, "Many years, but the tower was in private hands until the State took it over after the Second World War."

"So, there is no private property in Romania?"

"No." He smiled. "You know Proudhon said 'Property is theft'?"

I had thought it was Marx, but I nodded.

Bogdan went on. "Diana and I are employees of the State Tourist Board."

"Who owned this place before it came into State hands?"

"Ah, well. This Tower was one of the last to be taken back for the workers. It was owned by some Saxons called Brukenthal. But that was just a blink of an eye in the Tower's long history."

The crackling of the fire and the howling of the snowstorm outside filled a gap in the conversation. Then Bogdan said, "And now, about you?"

I shrugged. "I presume you got my details from the Department of Tourism?"

"Of course, but it is best to have it fleshed out by the man himself!"

And have everything go right back to the secret police, I thought, but I sat back. "Not much to tell. I'm a freelance journalist."

"From London?" Diana said, savouring the name of the foreign city as if it offered delights and dreams beyond the strait-jacket of Communist Romania.

"Yes. I'm writing for *Conde Nast Traveller*."

"About Dracula?" he laughed. "They always write about Dracula! And he was fictional! You should write about real Romanian heroes."

"Of the revolution?" I said.

From his reaction, he was indeed a was a loyal communist. No more jokes about the revolution.

I held up my hands. "I write what they want to read about, and what they'll pay for."

"And they will pay for Dracula!" Bogdan said. "You know this city is the birthplace of the real Vlad Dracul?"

"Sighisoara? Yes. Hence my visit."

"Very good. Now finish your wine."

But I didn't finish the wine. I engaged in pleasantries until I was a bit drier and then I went to my bed in the charming stone-walled chamber at the top of the Tower. There was a window with wooden shutters. I didn't open them because I could hear the wind moaning outside. I told myself that's why I didn't open them, but maybe it was really because I didn't want to hear muttering voices on the wind.

An old-looking ceramic heater had brought the room up to reasonable temperature, and there were thick blankets on the bed.

I undressed quickly, dragged on my pyjamas, and got into bed.

I slept remarkably well. The only incident was that in the middle of the night, someone woke me by playing the piano. I lay there listening, the soothing melody strangely familiar. Familiar, but at first, I couldn't place it. If anything, it sounded like an old air my mother used to play, but she hadn't played in years. She said she didn't have the heart for it now.

My dozing mind followed the tune up and down and round and round like the wheels of a water mill. And just as I was falling asleep, it came to me. That's what it was called: *Die Alte Mühle: The Old Mill.* But how had I known that?

IN THE MORNING, I ate a breakfast of cheese, black bread, salami and hardboiled eggs served with an indifferent coffee, maybe the best they could get. The local ingredients were excellent, and I enjoyed them. Bogdan and Diana seemed to enjoy watching me eat too. I felt like an exhibit in a zoo.

"And what are your plans today, Marcus?"

The shutters were open. I looked out the window. It had stopped snowing, but dazzling white rectangles of light reflected from the snow covered walls of the house opposite.

I said, "I thought I'd just take a wander around the town, get the atmosphere. I'm going to write something about Dracula's hometown, then and now."

"Sounds interesting," Diana said, studying me. I couldn't tell if she was serious. Her gaze made me uncomfortable so I sipped more coffee to avoid her eyes.

"I will come with you," Bogdan said.

"Well, you don't have to." I'd rather he didn't, but his bright smile suggested it was all part of the service.

AFTER BREAKFAST, we arranged to get ready then come down and meet up so Bogdan could show me around the town. I was down five minutes before the agreed time, as if eager to leave, but really it was because I needed to take a look in that big downstairs room where the fire was.

The fire was dead, but the smells of ash and old coffee pervaded the room.

The shutters were open, and sunlight shone in from the snow stuck on the walls of the houses to the back of the pension.

The front of the pension, through the shuttered windows I hadn't opened the previous night, looked over the city walls into the old graveyard.

Glancing around to make sure neither Bogdan nor Diana was near, I scanned the room, trying to remember what my mother had told me and what her father had told her: "To the left of the fireplace. Go to the wall and in the corner is a stone."

There was a whole line of stones exposed in the corner from floor to ceiling, and a wooden beam holder right above. But she'd said the stone we wanted was chest height and had a mark on it—a small diagonal line. She said if you didn't know the line was significant, you'd never guess.

I walked over and saw it, slightly darker in hue than the ones above and below, and there just below chest height was the mark, like it had been done with a nail, long ago.

I reached out with my fingertips and pushed. The stone shifted slightly. Though it moved, I wondered how I'd get it out. I only had minutes, but if I could do this now, then my mission was accomplished. I worked my fingers against the right side of the stone and dragged them but it wasn't enough. I'd need to work it out with more pushing and pulling.

Just then, Diana entered. I spun around, trying to hide the look of guilt on my face.

"Beautiful stones," I said. "Very old."

She looked at me oddly. She'd seen me messing with the stones in her wall, but instead of saying something, she frowned.

"I'm interested in architecture," I said feebly.

The tinsel on the Christmas tree sparkled in the slight breeze as Bogdan entered, muffled in hat, gloves and scarf, ready for the grand tour of Sighisoara.

Bogdan stepped into the middle of the room. He didn't appear to notice anything wrong though Diana was still frowning.

He beckoned and I followed him to the door. To make conversation, I said, "Beautiful piano playing."

We were stepping out into the face-freezing air, feet crunching on snow where only one man's prints showed. Someone must have walked around the tour in the middle of the night or early morning. I had the strange fear they were looking for me.

"Piano?" Bogdan said, interrupting me from my reverie. "Who was playing?"

"Well, I thought you were. Last night."

"No," he said. "We have no piano."

"But I heard music."

He shrugged. "We have no piano. Diana used to play a little, but not me. But still, we don't actually have a piano."

"Maybe from next door?" I said.

Bogdan gestured behind us to the Tower that stood alone in the city wall. "Luckily, we have no next door." Then he joked. "Just the cemetery."

· · ·

WE BEGAN OUR WALK. It took about an hour, walking through the city, past my little car, along alleys I must have walked, but couldn't remember. Diana haunted our steps, saying nothing, just watching like a ghost, or a spy. But Bogdan knew his history and was an engaging speaker. His tale was full of the doings of the good folk of Sighisoara and their battles against all enemies, with a large dash of Communist propaganda about the beneficent State apparatus that looked after everyone in the workers' paradise.

I persuaded him to take us around the graveyard. I didn't need to go there, but I wanted to.

"For the atmosphere, yes?" Bogdan said.

"Exactly."

The graveyard was picturesque, dotted with trees. The old tombs were overrun with ivy, whose green was now blanched by snow and frost. I nearly slipped once or twice as I tried to catch glimpses of the names on the many headstones. They were almost all in German. I only had the vaguest idea of where the one I was looking for could be. I began to despair of ever finding it.

I turned, giving up. No matter, he was long dead; he wouldn't know I'd been this close and not visited.

And then I saw it.

Johannes Brukthaler, Composer
Born 1872, Kronstadt
Died 1951, Schäßburg.

It made my heart trip. I gasped.

"You have seen something?" Diana asked, peering to find where I was looking.

I sighed, not meaning to. "No, not really," but tears welled in my eyes. I would need to cover this outburst of emotion.

Bogdan said, "Ah, you must be psychic."

I couldn't look at him in case he saw my tears. I glanced away. "Psychic? Why do you say that?"

Bogdan laughed. "This Johannes Brukthaler was the owner of the Schneiderturm before the State repossessed it."

My voice had a catch in it, so I stopped and cleared my throat before I spoke. "When was that?"

"1951. He died then."

Twenty-six years ago. I was four.

"How did he die?" I asked.

"I don't know," Bogdan said. "I wasn't around. But maybe it was his piano playing, you heard. They say he was a gifted pianist."

"And a counter-revolutionary," Diana said coldly. She was a fervent communist too. "A traitor to the proletariat."

Bogdan shrugged. "They say he was an agent of the West German Government."

"He was executed," Diana said coldly.

I wanted to punch her, but instead, I stood in silence until Bogdan said, "Come, there is more of the city to see. Much more."

I WAS EXHAUSTED by the time evening came. Nevertheless, I sat and listened to more of Bogdan's stories over a dinner of fried pork and potatoes with white wine. It hadn't snowed again, but it grew dark early, and somehow the atmosphere of cheerless winter clung to the old Tower.

Without them noticing, I wiped off the dinner knife with my napkin and smuggled it into my jacket pocket.

Later, I made an excuse and said I had to begin my article. I sat in my room, tapping away on the portable typewriter and managed maybe three hundred words, three hundred bad words. It was true. I did have a commission to write a piece uncovering the corruption at the heart of Dracula's Country. It was to use a metaphor of the blood-sucking Count and the blood-sucking Communist regime, so I had to be careful how much I put down before I got over the border.

I went to bed.

I had a plan, and I set my alarm clock for three am. In the quiet of the old tower, I lay there listening for that music again. I thought maybe old Johannes wished me well in my task. I dozed.

The alarm rang, and I silenced it almost immediately. I sat in my bed in the cold heart of the night. I had a flashlight in my suitcase, and I fumbled for it in the icy dark, switching it on with my thumb, the shaft of light setting motes of dust dancing in its artificial beam.

The room smelt cold. It felt cold. It was cold, and I was going to go downstairs in my pyjamas. If I got caught, I'd say I was sleepwalking or going for a drink of water in the kitchen or something, then meekly return to bed.

I padded down the stone steps and thanked Bogdan and Diana for the strip of carpet that ran down the middle of the stairs. Safely at the bottom, I crept through to the living room. A small fire still glowed in the hearth. It shifted and muttered as glowing ashes collapsed inwards in a splutter of orange and blue.

I switched off the flashlight to be less conspicuous and stowed it in the pocket of my pyjama jacket. I could see well enough by the light of the dying flames.

I wanted to be quick. I knew where the stone was now, and I had the knife to help me prise it out. I traced the mark on the wall with my fingertips. This was the one. I budged it slightly with my nails then slipped the tip of the stolen dinner knife into the gap, working it quietly, my heart hammering in case I was discovered.

I tried to prise it out, but it was still stuck. The stone budged, and dust fell from the crack in the wall onto the carpeted floor. It still didn't move enough though. I shoved the knife in deeper, really pushing it to get some leverage, and then I heard a noise.

I stopped dead. The only sound now was my heart pounding in my chest. I listened hard but heard nothing else and then something.

There had definitely been a noise. I listened again, wishing my noisy heart to beat more quietly so I could hear better. There was movement above, but whether it was the drowsy turning in bed of my sleeping hosts, or somebody wakefully listening to what I was doing, I couldn't make out, so I waited longer.

Then I thought: if I'm caught here it will be worse than if I'm caught on the stairs or on the way into my room. Best just get this damned stone out and see what's behind it, get my fingers on what I hoped was there, take it, and leave.

I went to it, digging the knife in as deeply as I could.

Ever so quietly, the door swung open behind me.

I span round, expecting the light to go and Bogdan, or worse, Diana, to be standing there.

But the light didn't go on. No voice spoke. Instead, I heard a piano playing.

The tune echoed from some ethereal plane floating just behind ours. The music went on and on, even more familiar now. It was ghost music—the ghost of a song my mother used to play: The Old Mill.

I had the strangest sense that the music wished me well and wanted me to get on with my task, so while the piano melody rippled on, rising and falling like water through a mill wheel. I dug at the stone, and it came free.

I had scarcely dared hope I would find it. I took the flashlight out and shone it into the recess behind the stone I'd removed. This was the hiding place I was told about, and there was the book.

It was a manuscript. I reached in and dragged it out. It hadn't been moved in nearly thirty years, and brick dust smeared the cover.

It was a manuscript of Johannes Brukenthal's compositions for piano, long lost since his death.

Johannes Brukenthal had some following in his life. By those who knew his work, he was considered a genius, but not much of his music survived. This manuscript of lost tunes was probably worth something, worth money to some, but worth far more to me.

I took it and placed the stone back. Stone dust littered the floor, and I pushed it around with my foot to make it less conspicuous. They didn't know anything had been hidden there. They certainly didn't know about the recess behind the stone; it hadn't been opened since they came to Scheiderturm.

My heart lifted in jubilation. My task was complete. I'd succeeded in the quest that drew me to Sighisoara. Now I just needed to leave, and leave I would; after breakfast, I would get in my hired Dacia and drive to Tirgu Mures. I put the knife in my pocket and set off back to my room.

The music stopped, but I didn't mind. It had given me courage when I needed it.

I was halfway up the stairs, going past Bogdan and Diana's bedroom door. My door was in sight. I reached it, grasped the door-knob and turned it quietly. Then their door opened like they'd been waiting to catch me red-handed. They might not know what I was doing, but there I was, the manuscript under my arm, a switched-off flashlight in my hand.

It was Bogdan. He sounded suspicious. "Marcus? What are you doing? Couldn't you sleep?"

I smiled. "No. I went for a drink of water downstairs."

"Oh," Bogdan said, sounding like he didn't believe me, but not having anything to confront me with.

Then Diana appeared over his shoulder. "What's that under your arm?" She pointed. It seemed she spoke a lot more English than she had first let on.

It was the manuscript. "It's my article," I lied. "I was working on it."

I realised it looked old and was stained with crumbs of mortar.

"You took it downstairs for a drink of water?" Bogdan asked.

I nodded.

Diana's eyes narrowed.

"Good night," I said quickly and walked on up to my room. I left the door ajar and sat in my pyjamas on the bed, the manuscript under my fingertips.

Bogdan and Diana's whispered voices could just be heard outside my door. They were arguing, probably about me. This didn't look good. Without a doubt, they had connections with the Secret Police. They were trusted people.

Anxiety tightened my chest. I'd got the manuscript. Not that the police would want that, though they might destroy it out of spite. The work of a counter-revolutionary couldn't be allowed to survive, but having a work with Johannes Brukthaler's name on it would be enough to tar me with suspicion.

They'd accuse me of being a stooge of the CIA or MI6. They'd send me to jail, and I'd be an old man before I came out again, if I ever did. I didn't relish the idea of years in a Romanian jail.

From their room, I heard the dailing of a phone, deep in the night.

I dressed hurriedly, throwing the manuscript into my suitcase. I was shivering, but as much from the fear as from the cold.

When I was dressed, I stood inside my door. I heard the phone receiver click down and Diana say, "They'll be twenty minutes."

I had to be gone before that. I would go and get the Dacia and drive. I didn't know how organised the local police would be. After all, this was a backwater. They might not have the hire car registration linked with my name. But even if they had, I'd drive and get on a train, a bus or a horse cart, and be gone.

I crept out of my room, and onto the short landing. Their room was closed, but light seeped from around the door. From inside, I heard Bogdan mutter, "We just need to wait."

Then I went as quickly and as quietly as I could and descended the stairs until I was at the front door. The key was in the door. I turned it, the metal cold between my fingers. I inched the door open, and when it was wide enough for me to slip out, I did.

But they heard me. The hall light flicked on, and Bogdan called, "Marcus! Where are you going?"

I ran.

Bogdan rushed out of the house and yelled at Diana to say which way she'd seen me go. Lights came on in the buildings that lined the narrow medieval alleys and shutters opened. I was now thankful for the sparsity of the streetlights as I fled along street after street and alley after alley, breath coming in clouds, slipping on the icy pavement beneath my feet. The sound of boots pounded after me.

This was their town now. They wouldn't let me get away.

I darted right—a dead end—then left: this was more promising, but I had no idea where I was or how I was going to get to my car. I needed to lie low. But where?

Footsteps and whistles sounded behind. I couldn't believe they still used whistles, but the shrill blasts pierced the frigid air. God knows how many people were behind, but I couldn't keep this up. My lungs burned, and my legs ached with the weight of my shoes.

I stopped for an instant, leaning on a wall, bent over, gasping for my life. I just needed a few seconds to steady my ragged breathing. Muffled sounds came from way behind. I thought of running again, but I didn't know where I was running to.

The streets around me looked both familiar and unfamiliar. The stones of the centuries stared down. I wasn't their enemy; my folk built these streets so long ago. And now I was back, twenty-six years after I was first forced to leave.

I couldn't out run them so I had to find somewhere to hide.

But I was just getting more and more lost. I thought of going to the graveyard. It was outside the city walls, but that meant I'd have to climb the walls. And first I'd have to find them. I couldn't see anything here just houses.

A whistle shrieked out ahead of me. A voice yelled, "He's up here," and was answered by one behind.

I was a fox between two packs of hounds. For all I knew, I might get beaten to death in a police cell.

In my agony of despair, not knowing how to escape, I heard the piano again. The same tune. It came from in front and right, ghostly and insistent.

But the police had seen my footprints. They'd soon be here.

The music got louder. What could this mean? Was some ghost taunting me? Was this the last trick of the spirit of Johannes Brukenthal, the composer? But he didn't hate me, and I loved his memory.

The shouts and whistles got closer. I was going to have to run again. But the music seemed to lead me, and I followed the notes that hung ethereally in the cold air between this world and the next.

The music drifted down from the alley to my left—a passage that looked like all the other alleys here. But no police whistle had shrieked from down there, and there was no sound of pursuing feet, so I ran down it.

The music grew louder. It surged, it fell, and it rose again. The haunting notes drew me on until I stood before an old wooden door.

But the house was boarded up. What was I supposed to do now? I pushed, but the door was locked.

The police whistles were so close, somewhere in the dark nearby. Shouts in Romanian, "He's near, look at the footsteps! They go down there."

My hunters were round the corner. The fox was nearly caught.

I prepared to turn and face them, prepared to be seized, then thrown into a cell to be kicked and punched and locked up for as long as they liked.

The music was all around me. I thought it had saved me, but it had brought me to this dead end.

The police whistles sounded out very close now. I could hear the excited yells of both police and citizens as they closed in.

Just when I thought I could not possibly escape, just when I thought their hands would soon take hold of me, the music opened the door. The piano notes caressed the lock and it clicked open. It clicked open, and I stepped inside.

It was an empty house, boarded up. A rat scuttled away as I came in, maybe more than one. The room smelled of damp and dereliction, but it was strangely familiar.

The music played, my memory wandered, and the police ran past.

I stood, shoulder against the door so it should not click open again and betray me. I didn't know how they couldn't hear the sweet melody because it was so loud. But they dashed past the door, blind to its beauty, deaf to its delicate notes.

In wonder, I waited while memories and images that for long years had just been ghosts flooded fully back. I had been here before.

The music rolled on, music my mother had played on her piano in our first house in England, music I now knew belonged to him, to her, but also to me.

This music had brought me into this house; my aunt's house. She was older than my mother. I remember mother bringing me here, huddling in tears while I asked her why?

They'd come to take him, she said. As a child I hadn't known what she meant. We left Sighisoara in the back of a furniture truck. My mother had friends in Hungary, and then from there, we travelled west to the border with Austria. After entering the free world, we went by river, road and rail through Europe and then from Calais over the English Channel, arriving into the shadow of the White Cliffs. I remember my mother in tears. For her, England was a place of opportunity, a place of escape. For me, it had been my upbringing and my life. But I always knew I had to go back to Romania.

I remembered my aunt, now dead; she never got out of Romania. In their eyes she was guilty by association with the composer. But we were lucky.

In a dream, I don't know how long I stayed in that old house, the blood of my blood, the flesh of my flesh, bricks and stones built by my kin.

Johannes Brukenthal stood against the Fascists and then when the Soviets came and installed the Communist Government, he stood against them too.

It's hard to say who was the most efficient at killing people, Fascists or Communists, but in the end, it was the Communists that got Johannes. They got him, but they didn't get his music. I had that, tucked under my coat.

Through a crack in the boarded window, I saw that it had begun to snow again, but I didn't feel cold. I didn't feel cold, and I didn't feel hungry. It was as if the music made me invulnerable to these things: an old man's soul, his indomitable will, his boundless love given to me now through his beautiful music. I stood spellbound. Hours passed as all his music played, and then the sun rose and light splintered in through cracks in the boards that covered the windows.

The shouts and whistles were long gone. I took my chance.

I stepped out, collar up, scarf around my face. In the daylight, navigation was more straightforward, and I found my way to the Clocktower Square.

I looked around. I didn't see the car, and for a second I thought they'd seized it, and I would have to walk, not that I would get far on foot.

A cold wind blew across the square, and I shivered, but then I realised that the lump hidden under a frozen white blanket was probably the car. The snow had buried the registration number, so they hadn't seized it.

The key was in my pocket. The door opened stiffly when I tugged it. I sat down, scraped the windows, and when I could see through the windscreen, turned the key all the while waiting for the police to come running around the corner. But the engine fired and eventually, the heater cleared the ice and mist and so I backed out, turned around and left Sighisoara, a town that was once home to my people.

I drove.

I didn't know if I'd get out of Romania, though I'd try. Every second was a nightmare, but I made it to Tirgu Mures. I planned on getting a train from Tirgu Mures to Budapest and from there to Vienna and the West.

At the West Bahnhof in Vienna, I heard the music again, but this time far away.

The next time I heard it played was in London. My mother lifted up the piano lid and for the first time in years, played. Though only two of us sat in there on that rainy day in England, there were three of us in that room, joined in memory, blood and spirit.

Johannes Brukthaler was my grandfather.

7

THE LIGHTS

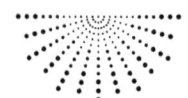

*J*ohn Hanley hurried to Euston Station through London streets thronged with last-minute Christmas shoppers. He pushed forward as flurries of snowflakes brushed his cheeks and shops were lit with Christmas baubles while passers-by looked with wonder at the white drifting feathers falling from a dark sky made orange by city lights. Ahead of him lay a long train journey to the wilds of Shropshire to spend Christmas with his ailing father, and he worried he'd be late. He had left the surveyor's office at Bedford Square around 4 pm, but it was already nearly dark. He had to divert up Tottenham Court Road to buy his father a Christmas present and card, which he planned to write once the train was moving. The crowds of people annoyed him. The sudden clumps of shoppers stopping to point in windows got in his way and made him sigh in exasperation.

When he got to the station, it was bright and busy. Spindly Christmas trees stood perched on top of the ticket office and the stalls selling newspapers and pies, their plastic branches hung with strings of blue, red, and yellow electric lights. John Hanley turned up his collar against the cold wind that gusted in through the open station entrance. As he got his ticket, John put down his brown suitcase. The case contained everything he needed for the days he would spend in Shropshire as well as the bottle of whisky he'd bought for the old man, in lieu of knowing what his father would really want as a gift.

He scratched under the brim of his hat as he looked for departure information on the boards. It was 1956 and would soon be 1957. He thought how little the dying year had given him and how much it had taken away. He sighed again. He would need to change several times and the journey would take many hours. He just hoped to make all of his connections and avoid spending Christmas Eve in a cold railway waiting room.

Just then, a woman came up to him shaking a tin. She smiled and said, "Season's Greetings. Could you spare a few coppers for orphans at Christmas?"

John Hanley looked at her stony-eyed. She repeated herself; as if unsure he had heard the first time. Finally, he said tersely, "No thank you."

Her face dropped. She was clearly unused to people refusing to help orphans at Christmas and paused as if thinking of saying something, but John Hanley had turned away. She shook her head and walked off, turning to brightly accost another man who reached into his trouser pocket and pulled out a few coins, which he pushed into the tin. John Hanley heard the woman give thanks to this stranger, but he did not see her move to the next for his train was announced and he hurried towards the platform to get on board.

JOHN HANLEY SAT by the window, facing the direction in which the train would travel. The carriage was busy. Opposite him, in the same compartment, a man and his daughter sat. She was excitedly prattling about Santa Claus and her father held her hand and beamed as he listened to her chatter.

Another man came in, medium height and heavily built, wearing a brown suit, with scuffed brown shoes. He took off his hat, placed it on the rail overhead on top of his case and sat down next to John. He made a harrumphing sound as he pulled out a newspaper then said, "Merry Christmas." The father and daughter grinned and wished the man Merry Christmas in return. John looked out of the window at the faces of those waving off their loved ones. Then he felt a jolt. Clouds of steam billowed past the window. He heard the guard's whistle and the train rumbled and moved.

"Just made it," the man in the brown suit said to no one and everyone.

The father of the girl nodded. "Don't want to miss your train on Christmas Eve!"

The man grinned back. "No, indeed."

"Far to go?" said the girl's father.

"Just to Birmingham."

"Far enough on Christmas Eve. We're getting off before that."

"Mummy's waiting for us to get home," the girl chimed in.

John Hanley had no book to read. He merely looked at his hands. Then he raised his head and stared out of the window, watching London disappear. The train rumbled and chuffed for mile after dark mile - through Metroland laid out in lights and paper-chains for the dying year, then through the Chilterns, past Berkhamstead with the canal boats lying long on the cold still water. Even they were decorated for the season.

The father and child got off at Rugby, wishing everyone a Merry Christmas as they left. John Hanley watched them go without speaking. When they left the carriage, the man in the brown suit broke the silence. "Lovely to see her so excited. You heading home for Christmas?"

John Hanley said, "No."

There was a pause, but the stranger seemed determined to plough on, so full he was of Christmas spirit. The man nodded. "We don't have kids. Wife never wanted them. I'd have liked a boy." He screwed his face up in a grimace. "But you have to accept what life gives you, don't you?"

John Hanley didn't speak.

"Do you have children?" the man in the brown suit said.

Finally, Hanley cleared his throat. "Yes. A girl."

The man smiled. "That's lovely. I bet she's looking forward to tomorrow. Will you be seeing her later? Or will she be in bed already?"

John Hanley met the man's gaze and said, "My wife left me this year and took my daughter with her." He said the words like an assault, an attack on the man for being so happy.

The man blushed, his fat face not knowing what to do with the news. He paused, gave another screwed up, tentative look and said, "Sorry to hear that, old chap. Bad luck."

"I'm going to see my father," John said.

The fat man brightened. "Ah, well. It's good you're not alone." He gave an awkward, sympathetic smile, but when John's face remained set, he looked away again.

Minutes went past. This time, John broke the silence. Still looking out of the window into a world reflected completely black, John said, "My father is a man like myself. We find it hard to understand other people. He was astonished I got married." John Hanley paused. "And I wonder if I did it just to prove I wasn't him. That's probably why my marriage foundered."

"I'm sure she loved you at first," the stranger volunteered.

"I'm just not very good with people," Hanley said. "I can't read them."

"New Year, new beginning maybe?" the stranger said. He clapped his hand on Hanley's arm, but John stiffened at this unaccustomed human touch, and the man took it back.

The man went back to reading his newspaper. John stared at the patterns in the material on the seat opposite. Nearly an hour went by. The man was filling in the crossword by the dim compartment light. John gazed out of the window. He saw the houses by the track with their tinsel and bright Christmas trees. He imagined the warmth and love in those rooms, and he envied it.

More time went by. Then the man in the brown suit looked at his watch and said, "We'll be in Birmingham before too long." He stood up and reached down his case and hat. "Don't mind if I go and stand by the door. It's nothing personal, just habit."

John said, "I don't mind."

As the man was about to leave the compartment, with his hand on the door handle, he turned and said, "Chin up, old chap. I know you've been dealt a blow, but things will turn up. They always do." And then, as he stepped into the corridor he said, "Want the door left open?"

John Hanley shook his head.

"Merry Christmas," the other man said and closed the door, leaving John Hanley alone.

THERE WAS frustration with a platform change but John managed to negotiate New Street Station in Birmingham and find the train bound for Shrewsbury. This train was emptier than the previous one and John guessed that many who were travelling on Christmas Eve had already made their journeys, leaving misfits, strays and the ill-prepared to fill these last services. At Shrewsbury, he changed again for Craven Arms.

Snow was falling heavily now. He could see banks of it beside the track in the yellow carriage lights. The empty countryside lurked on every side as the train made its way to where he would make his last connection. When the train stopped at Craven Arms, he was the only one to get off. The snow whirled around him and he turned up his collar. It was cold and dark. The guard's whistle sounded and the train departed leaving him alone on the platform. He caught the guard before the man disappeared into his warm office.

"Excuse me, when's the train for Bishop's Castle?"

The guard said, "It's been delayed. There's snow on the lines up through the hills. They're clearing it now but I'm afraid there'll be a wait."

"My father's expecting me."

"In Bishop's Castle itself?"

"No, near Clun."

The guard shook his head. "I don't think you'll get there tonight."

"I was hoping there'd be a taxi."

"At Bishop's Castle? At this time of night? To Clun?"

"It's been a long time since I visited."

The man shrugged. "You might be lucky. But there's an awful lot of snow down and they won't clear the country roads until after Christmas."

John said wearily, "Which way should I expect the train to come from?" He pointed down the track to the entrance of a dark tunnel. "That way?"

"Aye that's it. You'll see the lights first." He looked at John strangely, as if something about the traveller worried him. "But don't go wandering down the track."

"Why would I do that?"

The guard scratched his cheek. "A man killed himself in that tunnel. There's no chance the engine driver can see you to stop in time. I guess that's why he chose that spot."

John regarded him. "And you think I have the air of a suicide?"

The man shook his head vigorously. "I never said that. I'm not putting ideas in your head." He turned to leave, snow already covering his boots. "You'd be better off in the waiting room. At least there's a fire. And it might be a long wait, like I said."

John watched him leave and when he was gone, turned again to stare at the black entrance of the tunnel.

JOHN HANLEY SAT on a bench on the dark platform as if he was waiting for the snow to bury him. There was not another soul in sight. Behind him, there was a light in the waiting room but in front were only the covered track and the dark fields and woods of Shropshire. The guard hadn't put ideas of suicide in his head; they had lurked like a threat since his wife left him -- a threat or perhaps a solution.

He felt the cold on his cheeks and wondered what he had to live for -- a future like his father's, living alone since his mother died? He exhaled and rubbed his face with his hand. He was alone. He truly had no idea of how to relate to people. He was awkward in social situations, dull even. His own daughter preferred her mother's brother who was fun and knew what to say. Some people seemed connected to the wellspring of life naturally while every attempt John made to connect failed and he could see no prospect of it changing. He stared into the dark tunnel mouth - a threat but also a solution.

THE SNOW FELL SILENTLY. John was covered. He brushed away the flakes from his shoulders, but the damp was already seeping through his coat. He was freezing now, almost as cold as death, and the life in him shivered.

Time went by. The snow grew thicker, the night deeper. Still no train. But by now, he had little desire to go on. He imagined his father by the meagre fire in the living room, surrounded by the ornaments his mother had bought thirty years ago, which had never been moved since. The old man would be reading by the dim light bulb - some book about long gone wars. He would hardly miss John. He had probably forgotten it was Christmas.

He fell into a reverie, brought about as much by the seeping cold as any fatigue. His head lolled. And then a man tapped him on his shoulder. "I'm sorry to bother you, sir, but it's a terribly cold night to be sitting here. I almost took you for a snowman!" The man's humour didn't touch John but he lifted his head. Snowflakes dusted his eyelashes as if wishing him to sleep forever. The stranger extended a gloved hand. "Gowan Fell - pleased to meet you."

In a subdued voice, John said, "John Hanley."

"Are you related to the Clun Hanleys?"

John nodded. "David Hanley's my father."

"The surveyor? Though he'll be retired by now. I was a friend of your mother Mary."

"My mother?" said John.

"Come out of the cold. Let's go to the waiting room." Gowan Fell extended his hand to help John up. John stood, with difficulty; he was stiffened by cold. He dropped Fell's hand, but followed him, trudging through the snow towards the waiting room. Fell opened the door and John followed him in. A fire burned in the grate, glowing coals licked by blue, red and yellow flames. There were some wooden benches and a single spindly Christmas tree decked in cheap Woolworth lights. John could see the wire branches were wrapped in tinsel that had seen better times, but still the lights shone, blue and red and yellow, against the dirty cream paint of the waiting room wall.

Fell sat down opposite. The room was warmer but not such as to warrant taking off hat and coat and scarf. John wrung his hands to bring blood back into circulation and looked at Fell. The man had a black beard, half obscured by his scarf, and sad brown eyes. His forehead, such as it could be seen beneath the brim of his hat, was wrinkled. He said, "So, Mr Hanley, I take it you are visiting your father for Christmas."

John did not reply to that. Instead, he said, "How did you know my mother? She's been dead a long time."

"Thirty-one years," Fell said. He looked at his brown gloved hands, damp from the snow, then he glanced up and smiled. "We were sweethearts when we were young."

"So do you know my father?"

Fell nodded. "I knew of him. He came from Shrewsbury as an apprentice to the surveyor. I guess Mary chose a man with more prospects." He gave a laugh.

"What was she like, my mother? I was only ten when she died."

Fell's eyes brightened. "She was life. When she walked into a room, it lit up, when she left, the light died. Or so I thought."

"You were upset when she married my father?"

Fell nodded. "I thought I had nothing more to live for."

"They were married at Christmas, I believe," John said. This talk of his mother warmed him. It was true, she had been life: when she died, the light seeped out of the house and the things she had animated by her love became merely things again. When she was alive, the paintings she adored, the ornaments she decorated the house with, all seemed possessed by their own life, and when she was gone, it was like the sun going down. His father was not an expressive man, but how he shone when his mother was around. When she died, the old man retreated into himself and his dry books. He had sent John off to a boarding school and holidays at home were monotonous, until at the age of 17, John had gone to London to be apprenticed to a surveyor in his turn.

"Aye, married at Christmas," said Fell. "I wasn't invited, but I heard the wedding was a splendid affair."

John shrugged. "She's gone now."

Fell's eyes narrowed in concern. "Are you married yourself?"

John grimaced. "She's left me. I don't blame her."

"I'm sorry to hear that. Very sorry."

John said, "I'm sure she's gone to a better man - more lively. She said I was like a dry old stick." He rubbed his eyes. "I suppose I'm my father's son."

There was a silence, and then Gowan Fell said, "I sense a terrible heaviness on you. I wish there was something I could do to ease your burden."

John smiled thinly. "Can you change the world?"

Fell looked at him and then gestured to the Christmas tree. "Even in the darkest times, there is a light that never goes out."

John turned to look at the poor thing. "That? It should have been thrown out years ago."

Fell said, "When your mother married another man, something in me died too, I thought there was no light left in life. But now I see I was wrong."

John looked up thoughtfully. "It's a strange coincidence this, us meeting here, on what would be the eve of my parents' wedding."

Fell said, "It is strange. Here at the darkest time of the year, when all light and hope seems extinguished. This is the meaning of the tree. There is a light behind all things that can be seen, if only you look. But, alas," said Fell. "I did not. I hope you do."

John said, "You have kept the dark in your beard, for a man of my mother's age."

"I've been lucky," said Fell.

. . .

GOWAN FELL BECAME silent as if lost in his own thoughts. John felt the warmth of the fire on his cheek. He was tired. He drew a weary hand across his forehead. A gnawing emptiness grew in his stomach. The darkness swirled all around him. He looked at his hands - hands that could do no good, dry hands with no life.

And when he looked up, Gowan Fell was gone. He supposed the man had made his exit while he had been preoccupied with his black thoughts. He shook his head. What had Fell even been doing there?

He got up and looked at the timetable pinned to a board on the waiting room wall. The only train left was the one from Bishop's Castle, and that was delayed. He sighed heavily and stood. He left his case in the waiting room and went to the door. Standing there the cold hit his face. The wind had risen and it drove the snowflakes in a mad dance across the backdrop of the cold night. No stars were visible, just a blur of cloud, lying heavy like a lid on the world. There was no sign of the guard. All footprints on the platform had been erased by further snowfall. John trudged out over the platform, his shoes wet and struggling to make headway against the thick white layer. He saw the tunnel entrance ahead. It grinned dark like an empty mouth. He stepped down from the platform into the soft cold. The snow here was waist-high. He pushed against it, slowly making headway, moving from the platform lights into the greater darkness.

He almost stumbled across the rail, then found the sleepers underfoot. The cold bit him but he allowed his coat to flop open. He was shivering terribly, but he moved on towards the tunnel. He thought that if the train came, then it would strike him dead, and if it didn't come, the cold would end him. Either way, a finish to a useless life.

He went on. The going was easier now he had the wooden sleepers to support his steps. And then, the great half circle of the tunnel greeted him. The snow was less here, just what had blown in from the entrance. The rails became vaguely visible, guiding him on into this heart of emptiness -- his solution. The howling wind was behind but here in the tunnel there was a thoughtful silence. Nothing moved. If any living thing had been here, it had long ago sought another place. John Hanley stepped forward. And then, the darkness surrounded him. He stood alone with no reference point. He could see neither top nor bottom to the tunnel, only the deep void of darkness beyond imagination. John Hanley lowered his head and allowed himself to sob.

He walked forwards, hand in his hair, desperately raking his skin. He half stumbled then righted himself. He was not deep enough yet. Further he went, step after step.

AND THEN JOHN became aware of a presence in the tunnel. It was as if someone was there with him but they were the other side of a partition - present but not present, as if separated by years. And then it was as if he saw the silhouette of a man, darker even than the surrounding blackness. The man raised his hand, as if pointing to something that could not be seen or heard. John strained all of his senses, but there was just the deep silence of the tunnel, and then came the far off whistling of an approaching train. The man's arm was pointing.

John stood listening to the train. He sensed the man's concern. He was trying to communicate. The train got closer. The man was trying to tell him something. And then he heard it. It was like a shining out of space. The man spoke to him, but it was not about the train. He pointed, not to the oncoming engine, but all around. John imagined the empty interstellar wastes that lay between the stars. And in the emptiness, there was a music. He opened his eyes in wonder and saw the stars were singing. He heard the voice that lies behind all things. And in front of his eyes was the void and behind the darkness of that void an unseen light and out from this emerged stars - blue, red, and yellow, like the lights on a tinsel tree. In the darkest time of his life, when all hope was extinguished, John Hanley finally heard the stars sing. He guessed his mother had always heard their singing. The train whistled again and he saw the first illumination of its lights entering the far side of the tunnel.

But John stood entranced by the blue, red, and yellow light that filled him. For the first time, he knew the light had always filled him, just that he had never recognised it. In the darkness, there is light; there is always light. In that moment, John Hanley's heart opened and the darkness fell from him like the snow. He turned and fled the oncoming train.

JOHN RAN and stumbled in the snow until he got to the platform edge. He heaved himself up, struggling to his feet. Looking from his office window, the guard saw John's shape emerge from the dark beyond the platform and ran over to where he stood shivering. He stood there astounded, astonished to see John come from the track, so caked in snow and wet. Then he said, "I don't think that train's coming through tonight.

John span round to stare down the tunnel. "But it was there. Behind me."

The guard shook his head. "No, the track's blocked by snow."

"I saw it. The train."

The guard shrugged. "Then it must have been a ghost. There has been no train through that tunnel since the snow began."

John frowned and said, "I saw the lights. I heard the whistle."

The guard looked perplexed. He said, "I don't know about that, but I have just been talking to the wife. We only live down the lane. We've a bit of a houseful in for the holidays, but you're welcome to come and stay with us until we can get you off in the morning. Can't have you spending Christmas Eve on your own shivering in the waiting room."

"That's very kind of you," John said. He was about to refuse the offer, but then he paused and said, "If it's not too much trouble, I would love to come."

"It's no trouble, the wife loves visitors."

As the guard led him from the platform edge, John said, "Tell me about the man who committed suicide in the tunnel."

The Guard frowned. "Well it was about thirty years ago now, but the locals don't forget it. Apparently he was a well-liked young man, but his heart was broken, see? The love of his life married another.

Silly to kill yourself over that, isn't it? But I suppose at the time, he thought all the light had gone out of his life, and he had no other option."

"What did they call him?" John asked.

"He was a fellow called Gowan Fell, from Clun."

8

THE HITCHER

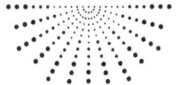

The snow came down like somebody emptying buckets full of frozen goosedown way up high. A glance to my left showed the sun had disappeared from the west behind the mountains and what light remained drained by the second from grey to blue to black. I'd been a fool to come this way, I knew, but it was the quickest route to get back on Christmas Eve and I wanted to see the kids faces before they went to bed. The quickest route normally, though now I regretted not taking the longer route by the motorway, which they'd at least keep clear.

Working on a Christmas Eve is the curse of being self-employed. I'd worked previous years but this Christmas Eve was snowier than any I remembered.

The windscreen wipers flicked back and forward, struggling to clear inches of snow as I peered into the gloom. I was in a rural area but just going through a village. Christmas trees sparkled in the windows of the houses I passed and people had hung snowdrop style lights along their eaves. I got glances of warmth and family gatherings as the atmosphere of Christmas deepened.

It deepened for them, but all that deepened for me was the snow. I knew I had to climb up to the pass and there was a chance I was going to slip and slide. I needed to be careful not to come off the road because hardly any traffic was passing now. No one as foolish as me.

I was out into the country now, leaving the lights behind me, cotton wool blizzards illuminated by twin tubes of light from my headlamps. The strain of concentrating was giving me a stiff neck and a sore head. If someone ran in front of me now, I wouldn't see them, and if I hit the brakes, I'd slide.

Then I saw a figure to the side of the road thumbing a lift. I did a double take. Was someone really out there in this? Where the heck were they going? But maybe they'd miscalculated the time and the weather just like me and wanted to get home for Christmas. Luckily I was going so slow that when I pumped the brakes I slowed at a steady rate rather than skewing off to the left or right.

The car stopped. The indicator lights winking harshly, the engine idling. Where were they? I twisted my head and peered right. I hit the button to wind the window down and with an electric whirr the cold and the wet came in. Feathers of snow invaded the car interior - winter ghosts that vanished as soon as they arrived. Still no one.

'Hello?' I craned my head and shouted again. 'Hello? Is there anyone there?'

I was just thinking I'd mistaken a snow shrouded gate post for a person and about to set off when there came a rap at the driver's side, not the passenger side with its open window. I felt a jolt of panic. The snow billowed in from the left as I wound down the right window, causing a cross draft of frigid air. Someone stood outside the car. I shivered, whether from the cold or from some primitive fear of winter ghosts, I don't know.

It was a man. I think it was a man. The figure stood tall and dark with snow flurries blowing round his hooded face. 'Thanks,' he said. His voice was deep and the accent local. That reassured me. He was a mortal man after all, one of my own people.

'Where are you going?' I asked, wishing he'd either get in or leave me to my journey.

'Just up the road.'

'Further on than the pass?'

He nodded. I could hardly see the gesture with the dark and the hood of his coat up. I was getting cold and keen to be on my way. "Get in if you're getting in.'

The dark figure walked round the front of the car, his legs lit up by each beam in turn. Then the door opened and he sat in, bringing chill with him.

I set off, pulling the car slowly back into the main carriageway, not that you could see it now, the snow was so deep. Nothing had passed me while I sat pulled up waiting for the stranger. And it was weird too how he knocked on my window, as if he was expecting to get in and drive.

I got up to maybe twenty miles an hour. It was going to take me all night to get home at this speed.

'You live locally?' I asked.

'Yes. Not far away.'

'Ah.'

Then he was quiet. As we progressed slowly up to the start of the pass, he said nothing and I began to feel there was something very odd about him.

After ten minutes, when we were starting to climb and the wheels had already slipped and shifted once, he said, 'Would you do me a favour?'

I hesitated, cleared my throat and said. 'Sure.' Then I laughed. 'Depends what it is.'

'Would you take a message to someone for me?'

'Well. I need to get back home, really. Sorry.'

He paused. 'You're going there anyway.'

'What?'

Despite the intensity of my concentration on the road ahead, I twisted my head. 'What?'

He was staring straight ahead, his hood still up. 'It's just a card. A Christmas card.'

I directed my stare back to the road. I couldn't lose concentration on this high, windy road or I'd wreck the car.

'What do you mean I'll be going there anyway? I have to get home.'

I felt him stuff the card into the pocket of my coat, uninvited with a muffled. 'Thank you.' Then a minute later, he said, 'When you see him, tell him I miss him.'

'See who?'

'Can you let me out here please?'

I looked at the whirling snow and the dark outside the car. 'Here? You'll freeze to death.'

'Here please. I can't go where you're going. Sorry.'

The guy was clearly crazy. I was glad to be rid of him. I thought he was foolish, but I wasn't going to fight to stop him. How could I? He would have to bear the consequences of his action.

I start to brake. 'Okay. I don't think…'

He interrupted me. 'Thank you stranger. I'm sorry it has to be you. You're kind.'

I really needed him out of the car now. He was starting to freak me out. He might even murder me out here if I didn't let him go. I would stop, let him out then set off again. Home for Christmas.

The door thunked shut and he was gone, vanished into the blizzard. Maybe he'd get a lift from someone else. Maybe I should call the police? Not that I had any mobile signal among these hills. Best I just get home. That was going to be enough of a struggle.

And so I drove on. The snow lessened slightly, but it was dark. I saw the entrance tracks to lonely farmhouses set way back down their drives, but then even they grew less frequent as I climbed up into the truly wild country. I crested the pass top, went by the cairn I knew was there from previous journeys but couldn't see now. Then I started to descend. If anything this was the more dangerous part of the journey. The bends in the road looked unfamiliar and I couldn't tell where I was. Then a sudden twist loomed in my headlights and I stamped on the brakes.

The car slid and swerved like a bronco as I tried to get control back. It gathered pace and fear shot through me. If I went over the edge here it would be the end of me. The car began a lateral slide and there was an enormous bang.

The next thing I knew was silence. The engine had died and it was cold. I must have lost consciousness briefly. I blinked, and shook my head to clear it. I couldn't stay in the car; I'd freeze to death, so I struggled to get out. I unbuckled the seat belt and shoved the door. It opened easily and that was amazing because when I stood outside, With my fingers in the dark, I felt how buckled it was. It was a miracle I'd survived at all. I pulled my coat in tight and turned up the collar. But weirdly, I didn't feel cold.

My plan was to walk down the road until a car came. So I walked. I walked for a long time and the night was so dark it was as if I was the only person in the world, alone in a realm of snow and shadow. And then I saw a lane leading off to the left. The sign on it needed painting but it said, 'Greensyke Farm.' It was incredible I could see to read because there was no obvious light source.

I figured I could keep walking on the road, but to be honest, who would be out driving in this weather? Or, I could walk down this lonning to Greensyke Farm. Farmers were bound to be in. And so I left the road and walked the stony path. My feet didn't slip on the snow covered rocks and soon I saw a lone farmhouse ahead. There was a light in the window. No Christmas decorations but a light there as if to guide travellers.

It took me a further five minutes to get to the farmhouse and once there, the snow blowing round my ears and face, I knocked on the door.

No one came. I thought maybe no one was in, despite the light. Then I reasoned that they wouldn't really be expecting visitors so I rapped again and this time there was the sound of movement deep within the house.

The rattling of bolts and opening of latches came muffled from behind the front door, then it was thrown open, not cautiously, but as if in welcome.

An old man stood there. 'You're here. I knew he'd send someone. He always knows.'

'What?' Shivers ran up my spine. Something weird was happening.

'Come in, come in,' he said. He looked and sounded like a normal farmer. They're so down to earth normally but this guy sounded as crazy as the man I'd given a lift to.

'Look,' I said, still standing at the door with the weather behind me. 'I just need to use your phone and then I'll be gone as soon as the rescue people come to tow my car.'

The farmer looked at me sadly. 'The phone won't be any use to you. But come on. The cold's getting into my bones, even if it doesn't bother you.'

And he was right. The cold didn't bother me. But at his request I stepped in.

The house was old fashioned. It looked like it came from years ago. I scanned around for the phone. I'd persuade him to let me use it. I'd pay him if I had to.

'Do you have the card?' he said.

My hand went to the pocket of my coat. I did have the card. He saw me move to it and said, 'Could I have it please?'

Without speaking, I took the card out of my pocket and gave it to him. It said, 'dad' on the front in rough, male looking handwriting.

Fear rose through my throat and mouth and eyes like a cold flower. I heard my voice falter. 'What's going on here?'

'My son David sent you. He always knows who it's going to happen to. That's why he gave you the card. He's never forgotten me even after all these years.'

My mind whirled. I remember stories about the myth of the ghostly hitchhiker. Maybe this was what this was. Except the guy hadn't vanished, he'd got out like a normal person.

I heard my voice waver. I couldn't ask this; it was too weird.

But the farmer smiled. He looked kind and at the same time sorrowful. His card was in his hand. I saw tears in his eyes. 'It's lovely,' he said. 'Was there any other message?'

I brushed back my hair with my hand. 'He said he missed you.'

The farmer nodded. 'And I miss him too. But it's just for a while. Until then he must use you and people like you to deliver messages.'

I finally worked up my courage. I had to know. I asked, 'Your son…'

The farmer kept smiling.

I cleared my throat. 'Is he…' I felt weird, but I finished my sentence. 'Is he dead?'

The farmer looked at me with a sad smile. 'No. We are.'

9

AN EDINBURGH GHOST STORY

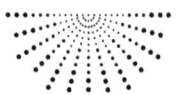

I went to the window and pulled back the net curtain of my upstairs consulting room to look down on George Street. The sky was white-grey and threatening snow. Snow was seasonal, I supposed, as it was Christmas Eve, and I had no need to have been working but I lived above the consulting rooms so sitting at my desk reading an old copy of Scottish Obstetrics Journal was preferable to whiling away the day alone. Knowing I would be there, Joan, my secretary, had come into work too, though we had no patients booked in. I had already decided to let her go soon today so she could get back to her family and prepare for the celebrations they would have in store for Christmas Day.

From the window, I watched the people and cars on the street. Among the traffic, a rag and bone man rattled by on his horse-drawn cart shouting out, 'Any old iron. Rags and bones.'

From the scene below, you wouldn't know there was a war on, but there was, even though it was far away. It was Christmas 1943 and so far there was no end to the conflict in sight.

I stepped away from the window and went over to the fire. The coals in the black grate glowed and gave off welcome warmth on that cold day as I stirred them with the heavy iron poker. Fire poked, I sat back behind my desk, but instead of the Obstetrics Journal, I picked up a letter from my daughter in Calcutta, received in October, and read it for the twentieth time.

'Dad,
    It's still very hot here. You'd think I'd be used to the heat by now, but I'm not! Luckily, I have the wardrobe for it now, unlike when I first arrived...

She chatted on some more but eventually came the words I guessed she had struggled to write:

Anyway, Dad, I might as well cut to the chase and say that, as antici-pated, Stephen and I will not be able to be back in Edinburgh for Christmas this year.

I'd expected it of course. Stephen was with the Fourteenth Army in Burma, and from the hints in her letter, combined with newsreels I saw when I went alone to the *La Scala Electric Theatre*, I believed him to be part of the Chindit force, operating deep behind Japanese lines. I put the letter down. Of course, I'd known she couldn't come home, but still felt the weight of it. Ailsa was a grown woman now, no longer the laughing blonde-haired infant that had brightened every day I'd spent with her. Now, she had her own life to live, and I had mine.

I raised the letter again, and read on. Ailsa gave an account of her life with the British Army wives in Calcutta that sounded very exotic to me who'd spent all his life in Edinburgh, born in the Old Town, educated at the University, trained at the Royal Infirmary, where I'd worked until going into private practice.

She finished the letter by wishing me well for Christmas.

'You know mine and Stephen's thoughts are with you this Christmas though it seems far from us here in time and distance and temperature! I can't believe that mother has been gone four years now, but I know she'll be watching over you. All my love, Ailsa.'

Silly old man that I am, I felt my eyes moisten at that. I would never get used to my wife not being here, though I do have faith and believe she is waiting for me for when it is my turn.

I put the letter down. Such a kind, thoughtful girl, my Ailsa, and both sad and ironic that I know the thing she wants most is a child but cannot seem to conceive, even with her father apparently the Scottish expert on childbirth and pregnancy.

THERE WAS a knock at the door and Joan popped her head round. 'Are you all right in there, Dr Craig? Would you like a wee cup of tea?'

I smiled. 'That would be lovely, Joan.'

I sat, lost in my thoughts until Joan brought me the tea in the Willow Pattern blue China cup and saucer and placed it on my desk, hesitating there a second until I said, 'You get yourself away now, Joan. Your family will be waiting for you.' This was the ritual for the past three years, though of course Ailsa and Stephen had been here last year and I hadn't been left alone.

She paused, as if worrying I would be lonely, but her family responsibilities called her. Looking away, she said, 'Well, I do have things to do yet. It's a busy time for women, Dr Craig.'

I smiled. 'Indeed, Joan. I have been told that many times over the years.'

She nodded, then stepped out of the room, returning with a small present, wrapped in red and blue paper and tied with a golden ribbon. 'Just a little something.'

I'd given her a Christmas box with her wages, and a card. I took the gift from her and said thank you.

She gave an apologetic shrug. 'It's nothing much', then laughed. 'It's hard to buy presents for the man who has everything!'

I considered the parcel and gave it a squeeze. It was soft — probably socks, or perhaps a tie. The man who had everything. She was right. I had enough money to buy myself what I wanted, though I didn't want much these days. Except the past, and I couldn't have that.

And then our brief conversation was done. I thought I caught a look in her eye, maybe of pity that I would spend Christmas on my own. But plenty of people had it worse than me. I was fortunate in my nice house on George Street, with a job I loved. I could have retired but what would I do with my time: Take up fly-fishing?

When she'd gone, I gave up all pretence of work and sat in my chair looking out of the window, warmed by the orange coals in my book-lined room. The sky darkened and the first flakes of snow fell as the temperature dropped. They drifted down like so much confetti, or the dropped feathers from the wings of angels. I thought of Stephen far away in the boiling jungle and Ailsa waiting for him in the wives' club in Calcutta. No snow for them. Then I thought of my Emily and the happy years we'd spent together. She was gone, but I didn't get regret anything in the closing years of my own life. I'd been lucky. I'd been happy.

And then I thought I saw something out of the corner of my eye. I jerked my head round, but there was no one there. Even so, I had the impression of a woman, and though I hadn't seen her clearly, I could have sworn it was Ailsa, dressed in a white linen dress, more appropriate for the Indian heat than the Scottish cold.

I stared at the space for a minute before telling myself what an idiot I was seeing things that weren't there. After all, I was a doctor, a scientist even. I dealt with reality and the physical, not visions and imaginings. My stare confirmed it. There was nothing there. My mind settled and my attention turned to the thickening snow outside.

I sat for half an hour or so, thinking nothing much, the strange feeling engendered in me by the imaginary woman gradually fading until the telephone rang. The noise was so unexpected after the hush of the afternoon that, at first, I stared at it on its cradle, as if not knowing what was expected of me. Finally, I shook off the thoughts that had occupied me and picked it up.

'Dr John Craig,' I answered.

'Ah, Dr Craig, it's Major Atkinson here, up at the Castle.'

I knew his voice of course. He telephoned more than most - always on behalf of his wife. His tone was almost apologetic as he said, 'It's Maisie again. She's not feeling so well.'

Maisie, his pregnant wife was a coddled hypochondriac of twenty-four years of age. She had treated her pregnancy as a serious illness from the day she first found out. I felt a sigh building, but stifled it. One needs to remain professional. Major Atkinson was a decent man, trying to do his best.

'She's worried that...' I heard him describe Maisie's anxieties, but he was probably worried too. She was such a highly strung young woman that she would be worried that she was going to die, or that her baby was going to die, even though she was in perfect health.

Finally, he said, 'I just wondered if you could come up? I know the weather is atrocious...'

I glanced out of the window and saw the snow was as thick as goose-down now and the light of day nearly gone. I said, 'Of course, I'll come, Major Atkinson.'

'All the way up to the castle.' He sounded apologetic. 'But I really appreciate it. Can I send a driver?'

It wasn't far. Around half a mile, I was even looking forward to the snow and the cold after sitting in the office all day. I said, 'Don't worry. I'll walk. The fresh air will do me good.'

'Thank you, doctor.' Then a pause. 'But please hurry.'

'Of course.' I could tell he'd rather I'd gone by car, but by the time the driver got here and we negotiated our way through the trams and last minute Christmas shoppers on Princes Street, I'd be quicker walking. And even I wasn't, I was doing him and his wife a favour and I was one hundred percent certain there was nothing wrong with her anyway so this part at least could be on my terms.

I pulled on my black woollen overcoat, hat, scarf, and took my bag. I was very proud of my shiny new doctor's bag. It had been a birthday present from Ailsa and Stephen. I had mislaid my gloves somewhere so went out with bare hands. As I left the room, I heard the ticking of the grandfather clock and the hissing of coals from. I hurried downstairs into the entrance hall, which was noticeably colder, and then the comforts of home were snuffed out as the front door closed and the cold Edinburgh air hit me.

The snow fell wet on my face as I stepped out. Already an inch or so had laid on the pavement and it crunched under my black shoes as

I went to the kerb edge. Cars and trams drove by while I waited for a gap in the traffic before crossing George Street. Once over the street, I walked down the hill to Princes Street running right-left in front of me. If it hadn't been wartime, Princes Street would be strung with Christmas lights, but the Germans had bombed the city and so no lights were allowed. There were lights in the shops though and the steamed-up windows glistened with tinsel and gaily coloured paper-chains reminding us of all the blessings of the Season while we waited for the War to end.

After crossing Princes Street I went into the gardens, by the National Gallery, aiming for the narrow steps that lead up the Mound and ultimately to the Castle. It was fairly dark now and there were fewer people around than I'd thought there would be. As I walked, feeling the cold, I pulled the collar of my overcoat up to keep the snow from falling down my neck, and gripped the handle of my bag, cursing my lack of gloves.

I went onto a less frequented way, finding myself walking alone. I went on, hoping I wouldn't slip in the gloom, but before I'd arrived at the steps, I had the strangest feeling there was someone there with me. At first, I ignored it, then I actually stopped and turned around to see. Of course there was no one there — no one following me, and so I walked on, reaching the bottom of the steps and starting to climb. I paused here and still no soul was visible either ahead of me or coming down. The sky was dark and heavy with snow and the flakes whirled around in the globes of the hooded lights. I stepped on the first step.

And then I heard a voice. 'Doctor, can you help us?'

I turned and saw an old woman standing against the bushes. She was bent with age and her face was lined. Her coat was in rags and strangely I could see her far more clearly than I ought to have in the darkness. I'd never seen the woman before in my life but I'd seen many like her — the Edinburgh poor, lots of them hard drinkers with heavy lined faces such as hers, though even most of them would be better clad on a night like tonight. The woman's clothes seemed wholly inappropriate. I paused, my free hand going to my trouser pocket where I knew I had a few pennies in change.

She raised a hand. 'Not money, doctor.'

I narrowed my eyes. 'How do you know, I'm a doctor?'

She ignored my question and spoke urgently as if she had no time for anything else but this message she must give me. She said, 'My daughter, doctor. She's with child. Her time is near.'

This was stranger still. How did she know I was that kind of doctor? But I had no time to divert from my mission to the Castle. I began to apologise. 'I'm so sorry, but I'm hurrying to see a patient. Can your daughter not go to the hospital?'

Very often the poor could not afford medical help, but in an emergency case, the hospital would accept the woman's daughter, if it truly was an emergency and not just a ruse to take money from passing strangers.

This was a more likely explanation, but still, I sighed and thrust my hand into my pocket, my fingers curling round the bronze pennies and ha'pennies. I pulled them out and for a second looked down to check how much I was giving her but I looked up, the woman was gone. Simply gone.

I glanced around, dumbfounded. Where on earth had she gone? I stared right and left up the path where snow was now lying thickly. No one, and no footprints other than my own.

I felt a chill of fear. What had I seen? How could someone vanish like that? But I had little time and less inclination to stay there pondering, so I climbed the steps, hurrying on through the soft dropping snowflakes and whirling darkness, driven by my appointment at the Castle, but also by not wanting to linger on that lonely path.

The cold cut into me as I climbed the steep steps. The snow was whirling now, half blinding. I shuddered, glad to be gone from that place where the woman had appeared in my path in such an eerie and unnerving way, but, I was breathing heavily; the steps were forbidding and my shoes slipped in the snow. The fingers holding the handle of my medical bag were frigid.

· · ·

EVENTUALLY, I reached the top of Playfair Steps and came onto Mound Place. An army vehicle had turned up the steep slope and was struggling in the snow, the wheels spinning and throwing up slush. The engine whined, the lights cutting through the snow and dark, but he was going nowhere. I passed by as the soldier got out, cursing his stuck motor. He ignored me as I hurried, passing under the row of high, dour sandstone buildings that watch over Edinburgh like cold-hearted prefects. Truth be told, I could hardly see them in the weather, but I knew they were there. The ancient forms of the city, normally a familiar and reassuring presence now seemed to whisper of ghosts and secrets.

Frozen, and wishing I had not offered to come and see the Major's silly wife on such a night, and Christmas Eve too when I should have been at home with my sherry, my fire and my book, I climbed the slope of Ramsay Lane. I was alone here, no one else was foolish enough to venture out. As I walked, my feet trudging in the snow, I fancied I heard voices. What an odd night this was turning out to be. Voices heard in the wind, half familiar, half strange. I rubbed my brow with three cold fingers of my free hand as if to erase such fancies and walked on.

The minutes seemed like hours, but at length, I turned onto the deserted Royal Mile. I say deserted but I could hardly see in front of my face to confirm that, but who would venture out in such a storm? The snow was deep, covering my shoes. The Esplanade before the Castle, normally so wide and splendid wasn't visible and could have been anywhere. As I shivered and trudged on, I could as well have been walking through the remote Highlands where no one lived. And then I reached the castle gate I found two soldiers there, standing in the sentry boxes that flanked the entrance, stamping to keep warm. Electric light bulbs gave some illumination to the scene, and I saw they wore the long grey greatcoats with their thistle buttons and the tall bearskins that identified them as members of the Scots Guards. Though I doubt I looked very threatening, orders made them step to bar my passage. I fumbled in my overcoat for the military pass given to me as a doctor attending the staff of the castle.

The one on the right took the pass and read it in the electric light.

'It seems in order, sir,' he said, handing the pass back to me.

'Here to see, Major Atkinson's wife,' I said by way of explanation.

'Shocking weather,' he said, his accent revealing him as a Glaswegian.

'Indeed, but very seasonal.' We exchanged pleasantries. 'How long before you finish?' I said to them both. I didn't want to linger in the weather, but they deserved some civility.

'Not soon enough,' said the other. A borderer from Dumfries or somewhere down there. And with that they let me pass, opening the small door in the heavy gate that led into the castle. Even passing through the gate, I was not inside, but I'd been there before and knew my way to the officers' quarters. Major Atkinson's batman greeted me and led me to their rooms, taking my snow caked overcoat and hat.

'You need some gloves, sir.' he said.

'You're not wrong. I lost them you see.'

FROM HIS SMILE, Major Atkinson was glad to see me. He shook my hand and led me through to the bedroom where his wife lay.

'Good evening, doctor,' she said dramatically. She lay in bed in her white nightdress, with her arm thrown across her brow like an actress in a silent film. Major Atkinson stood embarrassed, shifting from foot to foot until he finally said, 'I'll be next door.' I smiled, and he left.

I took out my stethoscope and approached my patient who had already lifted her nightdress to reveal her swollen abdomen for examination, her bottom half remaining discreetly under the bedsheet. I know from experience that patients like Maisie need to be treated with great thoroughness. It is not sufficient to do a proper examination, they must see that you're doing one. Not for them the quick and efficient, they want the whole show, but the good thing is that this is enough to quiet their anxiety in most cases. With that in mind, I fussed and pressed, and listened, and moved my stethoscope and pressed and listened again. The foetal heartbeat was normal. Maisie's blood pressure was normal and there was nothing of concern that I could find. Despite that, I asked her carefully about her symptoms, which when recounted were vague. I asked when the discomfort came on? Did anything bring it on or make it worse? How tolerable was it, et cetera, and she answered with big blinking eyes.

And then as I watched her tell me how she felt and saw the flutter in her eyes, it occurred to me that she was a very young woman, and this was her first baby. She was simply frightened. Her soldier husband had no experience of children either and what they needed was for me to reassure them that things were going well.

When I was done, I invited Major Atkinson in and said, 'I've thoroughly examined, Maisie...' I looked to her for confirmation and she nodded. 'Yes, thoroughly.'

I continued. 'And I can find nothing wrong. In fact, both mother and baby seem very healthy.'

Relief washed over his face and he broke into a smile. 'Thank you so much, doctor. I felt so guilty asking you to come out on such a terrible night.'

I waved away his concerns. 'It's my job. I don't mind at all,' I said, telling less than the truth.

'The least I can do is offer you a whisky. As a Scot, I presume you like whisky?' I was about to say I preferred sherry, when I thought a whisky wouldn't harm me, it might even fortify me against the cold I was shortly to venture out into again. No one was waiting for me at home, so I could spare a minute or two to warm up in his company so I nodded, and Major Atkinson and I retired to what served as their parlour, leaving Maisie to sleep, her anxiety relieved by my visit.

We sat in the old leather seats either side of his warming fire and he poured me a Glenmorangie. Handing me the glass, he said, 'Do you have children, yourself?'

I nodded and took a sip. When the burning liquid had made its way down my throat, I said, 'A daughter. She's in India.'

He frowned. 'A long way, but at least, you won't be worried about her fighting.' Then he had a thought. 'Is she married?'

I said, 'Her husband is with the Chindits.'

'In Burma?'

I nodded.

He shook his head. 'I wish I could have another crack at Jerry or the Japs.' By way of explanation, he said, 'I took a small piece of shrapnel at Dunkirk. They say I'm not fit for combat.'

And so we drank whisky, and talked of the war and children and fatherhood that comes with responsibilities, but such joy. I said, 'Having a child was the most wonderful thing in my life. It transformed me. I'm sure you'll be a wonderful father.'

A foolish smile came over his face, both flattered and scared. I knocked back my whisky, no point putting off my journey any longer.

I bade Major Atkinson farewell, and his batman brought me my hat and coat. Both were damp, but had been warmed through by being placed on a radiator. That was kind of him.

'You take care out there, doctor,' the batman said with a smile.

There was something in his voice that made me ask, 'Care? Why?' I put my arm in the coat as he held it out.

He grinned. 'They say the ghost has been seen again.'

I grunted, but was chilled. 'The ghost?'

In mock horror he said, 'The old woman. She appears from nowhere. They say she glows.' He was grinning, and I tried to smile back, but inside I was affected by his words.

He must have seen that I was unnerved because, without waiting for me to comment, he added, 'But I don't believe in that pish, if you pardon my language, doctor.'

And with that he showed me out, and I was in the snow again.

The same two guards stood at the castle entrance. 'Far to go, doctor?' The Glaswegian said.

I shrugged. 'Just down to the New Town.'

The other said, 'We'd get you a car, but I think you'd be worse off. They're stuck everywhere in this snow.' And in the little light from the castle entrance, I gazed out onto the freezing Esplanade and saw the snow was thicker. What vehicles had been parked there were now just heaps under white blankets.

Seeing my hesitation, but mistaking its cause, 'You could maybe stay here?' The Glaswegian said helpfully.

I shook my head. 'No, I'd rather get home.'

He nodded. 'Aye, you'll have family waiting for you on Christmas Eve.'

Even though it was not true, I smiled and waved.

The Glaswegian called after me. 'Merry Christmas, doctor.'

As I walked away from them, my foot crunching into snow, the other shouted, 'I hope all your wishes come true.'

My only wish now was to be home immediately and within half an hour, I would be.

As I stepped into the dark, snowflakes lashing at my face, I could hardly see in front of me and navigated by memory rather than sight. I was all nerves. Trying to shake myself sensible, I cursed my stupidity; I knew why. It was only my odd encounter which certainly must have an explanation, and then the batman's jokey reference to a ghost, but as I walked in that howling sightless white, fear possessed me — an ancient fear of the dark and the winter and familiar places made strange. Even in this city that had always been my home. I walked onwards and met no one, my head turned against the weather. But I peered into the dark, all the time fearful that the woman would come back. Irrational, ridiculous fears that the woman would indeed come back and that she wanted something from me.

Walking on, I passed the entrance to Ramsay Lane on my left, but I didn't take it, telling myself that it was because it was steep and I might slip, but knowing it was really because it was lonely, and she might be there.

So instead, I walked down the Royal Mile, a longer way round. Because of the blackout, all unnecessary lights had been removed so German bombers wouldn't be able to see the city from above. I trod my way carefully down the Royal Mile, all the time conscious I needed to cut left and make my way down the hill, but not wanting to take any narrow, lonely way for fear of whom I'd meet.

The snow was bad. I passed the odd pub, but even they had blackout curtains drawn and any cheer that was within, stayed within. I knew the city so well, but even so, after minutes of walking, I became disorientated in the whirling dark. I couldn't see, so I trusted I was going the right way, I was heading downhill at least and looking for any broad way I could take left. At the very least I would get to Bank Street and be able to descend from there even though it put me past where I wanted to be and would add distance to my walk. But it would be broad and I would pass pubs and restaurants — and possibly people — on the way.

But then I became truly lost. The city was my city no longer, and I did not know where I was. I felt my throat tighten. I felt my heart faster. I tried to keep it at bay, but fear spread through me like a weed. I walked rapidly and less carefully and slipped more, still gripping the handle of my bag even though my fingers were cold as dead bone.

I felt her before I saw her. There was no mistaking the unworldly feeling.

Everything around her was black, but I could see her clearly — a bowed, grey-haired old woman marked by poverty and wearing rags. Her dark eyes bored into me as she said again, more desperately, 'Doctor, please help us. My daughter is with child. I fear she will die.'

I felt words rise in my throat, half-strangled. I had intended to give an explanation of why I would not help her, but my words came out in panic. 'Leave me be, whatever, you are. Leave me!'

And, as if my fear-driven yell had power, the old woman faded before my eyes once again as if she had never been there. My panic took me over completely. The ancient terror of what is unknown, of the dead themselves haunted me and drove me through that terrible night. I ran, stumbled and fell, my knees wet with snow, snow in my eyes, snow up my sleeves. Once, I dropped my doctor's bag and fumbled for it, losing it in the dark in my fear, but finding it again, scrabbling for it, icy fingers grabbing for the hard handle, then stand-ing, running, slipping and almost falling again. I didn't know where I was. The place looked like Edinburgh of centuries previously. I despaired of finding any familiar street. If I came across a public house this time, I would go in and stand there, ordering a drink and then another, and waiting by the fire until my fear left me.

But I found no such place. I was as if totally alone in the city. Having nowhere to go cold and fearful I would fall and die of hypothermia on that terrible night, I walked and slipped on, planting each foot in front of me and forcing myself onward.

Then to my left there was a wide entrance to a close. I cowered away from that infernal mouth for fear of what might jump out and grab me, but in doing so, I skidded off the buried kerb edge and started to tumble. I threw out my arms to keep balance, but that only twisted me and my doctor's bag went flying. My fingers had been so cold, I couldn't keep a grip on it. I cursed my foolishness at losing my gloves; if I'd had them, my fingers would have been warmer and able to grip, but it was no matter now, the bag was vanished.

Rising from my knee, I couldn't see the bag anywhere. If it had been any other bag, I might have left it there unsearched for and come back another time when the snow and the dark was gone. But it was a gift from Ailsa, and with her so far away, its loss seemed a symbolic blow of ill-luck. I looked around, but I already knew where it had gone: it must have flown from my hand and landed and bounced and gone into the dark entrance of the close.

I sighed deeply. That was the last place I wanted to go. I thought again of leaving the bag and stood, reason telling me to leave and come and find it another time, and my heart telling me I couldn't bear to leave it when it would probably be found so easily just inside the close. The only thing that kept me from going for it was fear. I shook my head. I couldn't allow stupid fear to stop be retrieving Ailsa's bag.

I took a hesitant step towards the close entrance. Nothing happened of course and so, emboldened, I took another.

An old oil lamp hung there showing me that the snow had not invaded the close entrance but lay outside in heaps. I stared. A snow free place, once my fear was mastered, could this even be a sanctuary until the weather improved? A glance upward showed me that the close was roofed. Yes, if I sheltered here, I would be safe. There was maybe even someone here that would give me shelter. Maybe they would have a fire to warm me. And so I stepped into that quiet, darkened entrance.

It was a poor place. I could tell that as I stared into the gloom. Deeper in, another oil lamp hung, but at least there was no snow in here, and it was surely warmer than it should have been. I knew these closes of old. They were mostly gone now, knocked down or closed up, but in my boyhood, many had still existed. They had been the abodes of the poor: tenements where the impoverished lived piled upon each other, crowded in their hovels. Yes, this was a down-trodden ramshackle place, but at least it was shelter on this coldest of Christmas Eves.

I stood in the gloom there, waiting for someone to appear, but no one came. I looked around for my bag, but couldn't see in in the shadows. Maybe I'd been mistaken about where it had gone. Anyone living here was shuttered behind the wooden boards put up at their windows to keep out the drafts. I stood the mouth of the close, staring into the dark of trying to find my bag. Outside was the Royal Mile, though it didn't look like it through that hellish blizzard. It didn't look like modern Edinburgh at all. Still without finding the bag, I started to shiver violently. I was freezing where I stood, and tempted to venture further in where there would be more shelter, and maybe a degree or two more warmth. But the meetings of the night had spooked me, and I was fearful. and instead of venturing in, I stood staring at the snow, hoping someone would go past. Someone with a light that would show me where my bag was. Then I could tag along with them and their light until I found some familiar place and got my bearings. But no one went past and there was no vehicle that could get through that.

A noise came from the darkness. Startled, I stared into the dark throat of the close, and searched for the origin of the noise. At first I saw nothing, then deep within the shadows, someone moved. I started at the movement but then I tried to calm myself: Of course there were people living here, no matter how primitive it seemed, and these were my countrymen, no matter how far apart our stations in life. I called out. 'Hallo there! Who's there?'

No answer came, but I saw movement again. There could be no doubt that someone was there, for some reason keeping out of sight. I shouted, 'Hallo! Do you have a light? I've lost my bag.'

I attempted to sound jocular, but I felt far from it. The shadows rippled. Something in the movement unnerved me and I thought again of the woman who had appeared to me twice already that night. Perhaps she would appear again here for the third time?

And finally, a voice answered me. 'Hello there. Come into the close.'

The words echoed in the darkness and at first, I could not tell whether man or woman had spoken them. I hesitated then called back, 'Do you have a fire?'

The voice spoke back, this time clearly a woman. And a voice I knew. It was as if she had at first veiled herself and was now revealed. My heart thumped as the old woman called back. 'Come, doctor. My daughter is with child. She will die if you do not help her.'

She emerged from the shadows that ruffled as if she was stepping out of water dyed with ink, or wind rippled sheets of black silk. Standing now in plain sight, it was the same old woman in the close's gloom, a strange light illuminating her even though she held no lantern.

Fear rose, and I edged back out towards the snow and the wind.

She shook her head as she watched me move away. 'All of you have deserted us. All down the years, for we are mean and poor and beneath the contempt of folk such as you.'

I tried to reply that I was not like that, that I was a good man, but my mouth was dry and my tongue stuck on the words. I shuddered from cold and from fear. Then like a rabbit suddenly released from a trap, I turned and stepped away to the close's opening and the snow attacked me again, taking away my breath. I was almost free of her, one more step would take me from the close, and somehow I knew she would not appear a fourth time if I left her now. Then, from over my shoulder, I heard:

'You swore an oath, doctor. Once long ago when you were a young man, you swore to preserve life.'

Her words stopped me. Tension like a knife twisted in my chest. I wanted to flee, but what she said struck true. On the edge of white snow and black stone, between leaving and staying, pity rose up and contended with terror. She was right. As a medical student at the University, I'd sworn the Hippocratic Oath, all doctors did. This was too strange, too awful. This dilemma, this desperation was not mine. I had to go to preserve my sanity.

I turned to step again into the blizzard, but could not resist watching her as I prepared to go. Her old eyes were full of contempt. 'I thought you were a good man, doctor. But I was wrong. Let my daughter die. Go keep your Christmas Eve alone.'

Alone. But instead of self-pity that I would spend Christmas alone, her words brought memory of family ties and the bonds of love and loyalty that could not be broken, even over the miles to India or beyond the doors of death. And I faltered. I held myself in contempt for having thought this was only a trick to defraud me. Now, I half believed the old woman, whatever unnatural creature she was. Perhaps she did have a daughter. Perhaps her daughter would die.

She thought me a coward or a cold-hearted, privileged snob. She would let me pass from the close, but in that instant, I knew I could not deny her request. She was right. I was a doctor. I had sworn to preserve life, and not just the life of the rich and those who could afford to pay, but all human life. I thought of rich pampered Maisie with her doting husband in their castle rooms. And even for them I had pity. How much more should I have pity for this poor thing in her icy tenement.

Sensing the change in me, she pointed into the darkness of the close. 'My daughter is there. Her time is near. She does not have long. Help her before she dies like she has before.'

The atmosphere was dreamlike but, surrendering myself to what must be a dream, I said, 'Show me to your daughter. But I don't have my medical bag.'

The woman did not speak but pointed and where she pointed I saw my bag lodged against the wall. Stooping to pick it up, the handle cold in my fingers, I saw she had stepped into the close. I do not know how I could see in that inky place, but I could. I breathed deeply. I had decided to help her and her daughter and so, despite my terror, I followed her to the lowest and meanest of the tenements. She pushed open the rough door, and I sensed rather than saw a thousand poor ghosts watching me as she led me to a low room. On the floor was a wooden pallet that served as a bed and on the bed, heaps of old sheets and blankets. A young, red-haired girl lay there on them, her face pale and shining with sweat. She was far gone in labour but could not give birth. Her strength was almost gone, and I saw it was true what the old woman had said, this girl was close to death and I guessed that, without my help, the infant inside her would die too.

My mind reeled. How could I be a doctor to a woman in a dream, a woman who was only a ghost? Her mother watched me. She did not say, 'Can you help her?' but instead, 'Will you help her?'

So, I nodded. I set down my bag and opened it taking out my stethoscope. I listened to the mother's heart. It beat fast, like a trapped animal, but I could tell it was weakened and weary and would soon give in. The baby was twisted breach-wise in the birth canal. Years of experience came to my aid and with the instruments in my bag and my own hands, I managed to turn the baby. Sensing it had come free, the young woman pushed again, and the child was born with a cold wail. Instinctively, I checked my pocket watch to find the hour of its birth and saw that it was after midnight. Another child had been born on Christmas Day, in the early hours, in the dark heart of the year. Poor as the one we commemorate and born in such a lowly and mean place as He was.

'Thank you, doctor,' The old woman said. I have a memory of her showing me out of the tenement and into the close, but it is vague and ill-defined. I did not fully feel myself again until I stood outside the entrance to Mary King's Close. The snow had died down and only a few flakes fluttered now. The clouds had parted and riding high there in the cold grey sky was the quicksilver moon, shining down on Christmas Day. I knew where I was now and so I made my way down the Royal Mile, to Cockburn Street and over Waverley Bridge and home.

The moon shone down on the snow. The shadows were inky black, but where the moonlight touched everything was bright and illuminated in silver. A few revellers wandered homewards or to late-night parties. A couple of men wished me, 'Merry Christmas!' from the other side of the street, and then I was on George Street and outside my home.

I hung up my hat and coat and put down my bag in the hall. My fingers were frozen, and I flexed them to bring back the blood. Once again, I regretted not having my gloves any more. I went upstairs and found the consulting room was the warmest because it was the last place I'd been, but even so the curtains were wide open and the heat had mostly seeped out, so it was not warm, and I shivered again. I poked the fire and found one reddish coal under a pile of ash-grey ones. I didn't add more fuel. I didn't want to think and ponder. Time for bed.

I undressed and put on my nightshirt before retiring to the icy sheets of my bed. I lay there for a while, the images of my strange encounter running through my mind. And then I fell asleep.

I WOKE late on Christmas Morning. It made no difference; I had no one to wake for as I was to spend the day alone. I would have slept longer but there was a hammering on the door. Befuddled, I got up, pulling on my dressing gown that hung behind my bedroom door. I was so heavy with sleep that at first; I didn't remember what had happened the previous night. I hurried downstairs. The knocking came, more insistent now. Who could be calling for me in person on Christmas Day? I thought at first it must be Major Atkinson, but surely he would have telephoned as he always did. I frowned. Maybe he had tried, and I had slept through the ringing?

I would soon find out. I shrugged and arrived at the front door. I had put the chain across last night when I came in and as the knocking continued, yelled, 'Hang on a second. I'm right here.'

The cold air came flooded in, as I opened the door inwards. The snow still lay on the street outside and I shivered. A young man stood there in the uniform of the Royal Mail. 'Telegram for you, sir,' he said, thrusting the envelope into my hand and turning with a 'Merry Christmas,' before heading on down the street. I was bemused as I stepped in and closed the door to keep out the cold. Standing there in the hall, I opened the envelope. It was from Ailsa.

DAD, WISH I WAS HOME WITH YOU FOR CHRISTMAS. BUT GOOD NEWS! I AM TO HAVE A CHILD!!! AILSA.

I read the telegram again, a strange wonder filling me. With a broadening smile on my face, I thought of my beloved daughter so far away. Her wishes and prayers had been answered. After trying and failing so long, she was finally to have a child. And standing there, in that cold entrance hall, I wondered whether my service to the old woman and her daughter had anything to do with that.

A broad smile on my face, I wandered back to my consulting room and my eye caught the present that Joan had given me before she left on Christmas Eve. Putting down the telegram, I opened the bright wrapping paper and found that Joan had given me a pair of gloves.

ABOUT THE AUTHOR

Tony Walker is the producer of The Classic Ghost Stories Podcast and author of several books of ghost and horror stories.

ABOUT THE AUTHOR

ALSO BY TONY WALKER

Christmas Ghost Stories

More Cumbrian Ghost Stories

Further Ghost Stories

Haunted Castles

London Horror Stories

Horror Stories For Halloween

www.ingramcontent.com/pod-product-compliance
Ingram Content Group UK Ltd.
Pitfield, Milton Keynes, MK11 3LW, UK
UKHW020413030126
9848UKWH00087B/1157